After it Happened

Book 4: Hope

Devon C Ford

VULPINE
PRESS

Originally self-published by Devon C Ford in 2016

Published by Vulpine Press in the United Kingdom in 2017

ISBN: 978-1-910780-30-5

www.vulpine-press.com

Dedicated to my own symbol of hope.

My daily dose of happiness.

My H.

PROLOGUE

Steve's return trip was a lonely one. The two hours spent airborne to deliver the advance party was enjoyable as he guided the huge machine over the landscape.

Their target wasn't difficult to find: the protected bay was unique in its geography and rich in lavish houses. Row upon row of individually sculpted residences, each with their own private jetty leading to the calm waters, jutted out over the high ground.

They called it "Million Row," which was ironic because you'd have been very lucky to buy a house there with a measly one million.

Just before midday, he had swooped low to a patch of clear, open ground to allow his two passengers to jump from the side door and run for cover after closing the fuselage door behind them.

Steve had been on the ground for no more than a few seconds before his feet and hands guided the green Merlin helicopter upwards in a surge of power.

He turned the nose north, dipped it low and screamed away over the rooftops.

Without someone with him to focus his mind, his thoughts wandered, as they often did. He found himself again having covered miles in the air travelling in excess of one hundred and sixty miles an hour without any conscious thought. He had to stop doing that.

His focus returned to the immediate when he was about forty miles out and a blinking red light above his head became the centre of his world: oil pressure warning.

He tapped the readout in the vain hope experienced by every human being in such a situation that it might just be a mistake. It wasn't. He began to feel a subtle change in the way his bird was holding the air – a slight tug here and there, more effort needed to keep her straight.

His fears of the diminished lifespan of a modern aircraft without proper maintenance was becoming fact all too quickly. He faced a difficult decision: make distance towards home as fast as possible or slow down and be prepared to ditch the aircraft at a slower speed which wouldn't necessarily result in a violent death.

He steadied his nerves, opted for a period of speed and prayed he would make it back.

THE COMMON DENOMINATOR

Marie's revelation prompted mixed feelings in Dan. He was utterly overjoyed at the knowledge that she was pregnant, and in the same second terrified that she would die. He felt utterly distraught that their baby would never live.

Being the well-adjusted and emotionally open man that he was, his fear and concern presented themselves as an impotent anger.

This did not impress Marie.

He tried to comfort her, to wrap her up in his arms and recite false platitudes like "it's going to be OK", but he couldn't force himself to lie convincingly. Even for her.

He found himself avoiding her, furthering the distance they felt growing between them. He had to do something. Every problem had at least one solution, and if something couldn't be immediately fixed with action, then he had no idea what to do or where to even start.

He stalked from room to room, looking for some useful activity or distraction to present itself. He found Kate sitting with Sera in the lounge and stopped. He wanted to confide in Kate, but Sera always mocked him and provoked arguments; he knew it was just their personalities clashing, but he couldn't deal with that right now.

He mumbled to Kate, asking for a word. A scathing look was fired at him from Sera, and the two disentangled themselves as Kate rose. She walked with him outside, waiting patiently as he directed Ash off to search the bushes and lit himself a cigarette.

"Marie's pregnant," he said finally.

No look of joy washed over her face as such revelations usually prompted. The memory of delivering stillborn babies and fighting frantically to save the lives of their mothers was still a raw nerve for her. She knew what the news meant better than most.

"Before you say it was irresponsible, it happened before we knew about the problems. She reckons she's about five weeks gone," he said, looking at the floor and feeling utterly to blame for putting her life in danger.

"We'll do everything we can for her," Kate replied, placing a reassuring hand on his shoulder and feeling his pain for the impending loss.

"Everything," Dan said with a mirthless smile. "What more can be done than to just try and keep her alive? An abortion?"

He felt instantly wretched for saying it out loud, but he couldn't help thinking that it was early enough for her to take something and stay alive at the cost of their baby. He stopped and screwed his face up to try and keep the fear and grief locked inside.

Kate surprised him then, wrapping him up in a big hug while telling him it was going to be OK. He wanted to believe her. He almost did. How was it so easy for some people to comfort others, but his attempts just made them angry?

"We'll look at this again from scratch. Go over all the medical histories and find something," she said as she let him go.

He mumbled his thanks as she turned and walked back to the house. He stayed outside, letting the late summer morning warm his body.

Ash snapped his head up and stared as two figures approached, jogging down the long driveway. No growl came from him, betraying that he already knew their identities when Dan couldn't tell from that distance other than to guess. He glanced up at his master, who nodded his head towards the two runners. As Ash bounded away to greet them, the shapes became two slim young women.

Leah had taken to running with Emma, the two pushing each other further and faster each time. Emma wanted to run, and a simple compromise to keep her safe was for his lethal protégé to accompany her.

They raced each other the last hundred yards, Ash excitedly bounding along with them and keeping pace with little effort. Leah pulled up in front of Dan a clear ten paces ahead of Emma and stood smiling while she caught her breath.

Leah saw his face and stopped smiling.

"What?" she asked, her chest heaving to replace the oxygen used on the sprint finish.

Dan just shook his head, unable and unwilling to open the floodgates to his feelings right now. He went to turn away and was stopped by Leah.

Less than eighteen months ago, she was a scared young girl, but now she was a frightening young woman. She was fit and strong, and skilled with guns and knives, as well as fearsome when unarmed. He trusted her, and she had repaid all his efforts with unwavering loyalty and flattered him with imitation.

"Hey!" she snapped at his back, demonstrating that she also bore no small resemblance to Marie's strength of character. "What's going on?" she tried again.

Dan weighed up his responses, knowing that she would not let it lie until she found out what was troubling him. "Marie's pregnant, and I'm terrified I'll lose her," he said simply, only just managing to keep his voice from cracking.

Leah threw her arms around him and held on tight, unable to voice her feelings. Marie and Dan were her mentors, her role models, effectively her parents.

Emma stood awkwardly aside waiting for their moment of emotion to pass, her analytical brain seeking any solution that could ease the all-too-evident pain in Dan to whom she owed so much, including her life. "We can start again from the beginning," she said quietly, unknowingly echoing Kate's words, "find anything, anything at all, that we have in common. There has to be a reason we are immune. There has to be a common denominator."

With that, her eyes glazed slightly as she delved deep into her thoughts. She walked back to the house, her pace gathering as she went.

NEEDLE IN A HAYSTACK

"Well, that's probably not that accurate," explained Emma unhelpfully. "It's more like looking for a needle in a haystack, but when we don't know what a needle is, what it looks like or what it's made of."

The assembled blank faces made her instantly regret speaking out loud after Kate had voiced her opinion on the gravity of their task. Emma still felt awkward around people in general but was learning to find common ground with some. Since leaving university, she had spent almost no time at all with others who weren't also scientists.

Dan rubbed his eyes, no longer bothering to try and hide the strain he felt. Marie snaked a hand over his shoulders to reassure him in a gesture that was typical of her manner. She seemed less worried about it than he was, or at least that was what she portrayed. She was oddly fatalistic about it; "what will happen will happen," she said. It was inexorable.

Dan outright refused to sit back and accept that fate held any sway over him; he believed that your own future was decided by your actions and not some divine intervention. If he didn't like the way something was turning out, then he changed it.

He leaned back to her, accepting some small comfort in her touch as Kate and Emma discussed possibilities, getting them nowhere.

"The way I see it," he said, silencing them all out of pure interest, "is that there has to be one thing which we all have in common. I'm no scientist, but I've investigated enough things in my life to know that wild theories aren't going to make a difference to anyone. Emma, what did you say the factors were?"

She seemed a little confused at having to explain base-level virology and immunology to the group, but dutifully responded.

"Genetic, synthetic, environmental," she said.

"So," Dan said, allowing the exhaustion he felt to show as annoyance, "every single one of us has one of those things in common somewhere. Re-interview everyone, get a deeper history. Did they have any illnesses as a child, for example?"

"Well, I've barely had more than a cold since I ended up in hospital on holiday," offered Marie to get the ball rolling.

"Same here," said Kate. "The only time I've been properly ill was from antimalarial tablets."

"Urgh," said Dan, shuddering, "Lariam. That stuff made us all rotten on deployment; typical Army and their cheap medicine. Most of the guys threw theirs out and took their chances with malaria instead."

"The Doxycycline they gave us wasn't much nicer," said Emma quietly.

Silence hung in the room as the coincidences began to connect, like a domino run had just been toppled.

"Are you fucking kidding me?" said Kate, marvelling at how offensively simple a solution had just presented itself.

"OK," said Emma, scrabbling through the mess on the table for a pad and pen, "where did you go, when, and what vaccinations or medications did you take?"

"Mid-1990s. Kilimanjaro expedition via Nairobi. Lariam and some injections, but I never thought to ask what," said Dan, suddenly more awake at the possibility of a new line of enquiry.

Emma turned to Kate.

"Ethiopia. Ten years ago, medical outreach charity work. Doxycycline," Kate said.

"Viral research centre in Uganda," Emma said to herself, following up with, "ironic."

All eyes turned to Marie.

"Safari. Kenya, six or seven years ago now. No idea what I had, but it was injections before I went and a tablet every day which made me feel like shit, so I stopped taking them," she said simply.

Kate stood and threw open a filing cabinet, snatching a list of all the names of their residents and throwing pages at her team and including Emma in the distribution.

"Travel history. Dates, places, medication. Go!" Kate said, scattering them from the room. She sat heavily and looked at the only two people still in the room.

She saw a scarred warrior, a man she had seen take so much physical abuse over the last year and a half that she was amazed he still functioned. A ruthless killer when pressed but doggedly loyal to his cause and a more chivalrous man than she had ever met. Even if he was emotionally retarded. Next to him was a fierce and domineering woman with a natural ability to lead and control others. They were the Alphas of this small clan.

Only now they looked like a pair of tired children trying to put on brave faces to avoid being sent to bed.

Marie's mask slipped back into place first. She sat herself up, smiled at Kate, and spoke with renewed confidence. "Seven months to figure this out, then! Come on, knobhead, let's get me a cup of tea; you never told me you climbed Kilimanjaro!" she said kindly to Dan, prompting him to wake up as intended by the comedy insult.

"You never asked," he replied.

He stopped at the door and turned back to look at Kate. She gave him a nod of reassurance and watched him follow his woman.

THE NEEDLE

"Without a doubt, it's our only lead. Everyone has some link to Africa, the various inoculations for travelling there, or antimalarials," said Emma after going over all of the information again.

As per one of her various idiosyncrasies, she had collated this information into charts on her laptop. After consulting a world atlas courtesy of Pip in the library, she presented that the majority had visited – or planned to visit – Africa or a very nearby island within the last fifteen years.

Dan recalled Penny telling him once that she had taught children English in Gambia on a trip as part of a school exchange. Neil had responded with his own exploits as a young soldier on his first trip abroad. Quite how they didn't realise then that it was such a coincidence to have all visited an uncommon destination escaped him, but then they had other things on their minds at the time.

Like surviving the next twenty-four hours.

Slightly annoyed at the unnecessary PowerPoint display, Dan cut her off as politely as possible. "So basically that's all we know. But the Ugandan viral research centre sounds like a pretty good bet to me," he said.

"Six and a half thousand miles to the equator, with two oceans to cross and no guarantee of transport other than walking for most of the journey," said Steve after clearing his throat.

"Technically, it's a channel and sea…" said Emma, not grasping that it was the rhetorical instead of the literal being discussed. Her voice trailed off as she realised her mistake in speaking again.

"I understand why, but it's a ridiculous risk to try and make that journey," Steve said, fixing Dan with a look of challenge.

"Do you?" Dan snapped back, more harshly than he intended. "You really understand why I'm suggesting making a probably ten-thousand-mile journey with countless variables with a pregnant woman?"

Steve sighed. He'd seen that fire in Dan's eyes before. Seen it after he had burned a group of attackers alive in a barn, gunning down anyone who ran, and strung up their leader in bloody revenge. There were many things he saw eye to eye with the younger man about, but this was not going to be one of them.

"Needs of the many, my friend," Steve said as he stood.

Dan nearly flipped. The needs of the many were irrelevant to him now; the human race would die out in the existing generation if the answers he desperately sought weren't found.

His mind was made up. He was making this journey, and he would get Marie there before she was due to give birth if he had any hope of saving their child.

He said nothing. Instead, he turned and walked from the room lest he say something to a loyal friend he would later regret. He snapped his fingers aggressively, prompting his huge dog to rise from the floor with a grumble and lope outside to follow him.

He lit a cigarette and paced restlessly. He wanted to break something. He needed to act; he saw no other way of fixing a problem. For the last year, everything that had stood in the way of success could be fought and killed. Now he felt powerless. Useless.

Steve followed him outside and bent to stroke Ash between the ears. "I do get why you want to go," he said quietly, "but you can't drag everyone literally halfway across the world on a hunch. People are settled here. They're happy and they're safe. They will want to stay. I'll help however I can, but I can't abandon what we've built here."

With that, Steve turned away and went back inside.

Dan was left brooding. Who would follow his wild goose chase? Did he really think he held enough sway over the group? Did he command enough loyalty and respect to potentially condemn others by following him into uncertainty?

There was only one democratic way to find out. He would spread the facts among the group and see if he had enough support to make it viable.

A TEST OF LOYALTY

He decided that the best way to announce the plan was to put up notices and encourage people to make their own decisions.

He and Leah copied their proposal out onto large pieces of paper and hung them in the dining hall for all to see. A brief announcement over breakfast the next morning got the group clamouring to read this latest development.

The note was simple enough. Studies of the group's immunity showed a link to Africa in some form. Dan proposed an expedition there to find out if they could solve the problem of having stillborn babies. It was a long shot, but it was a chance to perpetuate the human race.

Anyone wanting to volunteer, or to know more, could come and see him.

The response was not what he was expecting.

Maybe Steve had read the signs right before Dan opened his mouth. Maybe the older man's experience gave him more perspective. One thing was for certain: the majority of the group turned their back on him.

They saw it as desperate, as him abandoning them. There was outcry that he would take away their guns, their protection, and leave them all to the mercy of dangerous people. They conveniently forgot that it was Dan who had nullified every serious threat within hundreds of miles. Dan who had found this place, cleared it, guarded it and defended it against attack twice over.

Ungrateful bastards, he thought.

But they weren't; they were just scared.

Marie, despite her positivity, was anxious that the trip happen. She had to do everything in her power to ensure that her baby lived, and that included making the journey to get any answers she could. There had to be a way, and until she had exhausted all options, then she wouldn't give up. Her change in attitude betrayed that she desperately wanted the baby, and her fatalistic opinions were for the benefit of others and not herself.

She tried to convince herself that she wasn't going stir-crazy from having barely left the prison in almost a year. She longed to be out – but not by only going on short trips under protection. She would be stuck here until she died otherwise.

The loyalty of others was their sole reason for volunteering. Leah was the first to say she was going, and Dan didn't even try to convince her to stay at home and hide in relative safety. He loved that girl, and having seen her grow up ten years' worth in twelve months wasn't the only reason. She had become a fearsome addition to his fighting strength, and going without her would be like going without Ash.

Neil announced in a characteristic comedy accent that he was becoming soft and felt the need for some fresh air. In all the time Dan had known the man, Dan had never seen him take anything seriously. He knew that beneath the poor humour and the extravagant impressions lay a serious mind, but his oldest living friend was a dependable and capable man.

He had two guns and a mechanic to accompany his pregnant woman – not enough for a scavenging run, let alone a journey taking months.

Slowly, and as inexorably as the tide turning against him by the majority, others came forward.

Jimmy was another man loyal to Dan. He was resourceful and kind with a sharp intelligence which had proven itself valuable on many occasions. Dan asked him if he would be OK leaving Kev behind.

"Kev will be fine. He didn't cope well with the outside world, but he's busy and happy now. He's fed and he has work to do. That's all he wants. Plus, Maggie has him under her wing."

Dan nodded as he absorbed this. Kev was a giant man, hugely strong but with a child's mind. The acquired brain injury he'd received at birth left him with a very simple understanding of life. The dead bodies littering the world in the aftermath of the pandemic had made him weep out of fear and a lack of knowledge. Kev was safe and happy now, and Maggie and Cedric had moved him into their home a short distance away on the gardens. He was given a good breakfast every morning, worked tirelessly all day, then sat happily in the evening as Maggie read to them both. He was happy, and Jimmy could finally let go of the need to protect him.

Jack, his grizzled old Belfast lorry driver, was another restless soul who trusted Dan with his life. He made a great deal of noise about how he was old but still useful, and could drive anything with wheels. Dan would never had precluded him on the basis of age; he was like a fit old billy goat and would probably outlive them all.

Adam and Laura were surprise candidates, both expressing a wanderlust and relishing the chance to be a part of something life-changing. Lou, his ever-reliable seamstress and lover of gossip, came forward to ask to join. She was somewhat self-effacing, saying that she had little to offer in terms of skills, but said that people needed organising, repairs to clothes needed to be made, and coffee needed brewing.

Pip, the tiny young girl rescued from the grasp of Bronson's gang, wanted to know more. She had lost a child not long after it happened, and that loss and longing could never be satisfied unless she found out if there was anything that could have been done.

Their newest Ranger, Mitch, had a soldier's thirst for adventure, nothing more and nothing less. If they were going interesting places, then he was in. Most people's idea of hardship seemed like a class upgrade for him.

One sad addition to the party was Ana. Since losing her baby and almost her life some months ago, she had withdrawn from Chris. They now lived in separate rooms, as neither could fully come to terms with what had befallen them. Dan thought it was likely she was leaving the pain of the memories behind and doubted whether she would want to return.

APOLOGY ACCEPTED, TRUST DENIED

There was no going back after the announcement had been made. Even if the whole expedition was abandoned, then many people wouldn't trust that Dan would stay in the long run. He had sealed his own fate, and also those of many of the group.

He had twelve people on his side, and of those, only four trigger fingers including himself. He also had no medical personnel bar his own and Leah's training.

Lexi had been torn but stuck to her principles and refused to leave home, as had Steve. The older man was to take over as Head of Operations, just as Mike was to replace Neil on the council. The headship of Logistics was open but would no doubt either be filled or swallowed up by Supplies and come under Andrew's control.

Lexi wanted to stay primarily for Paul, and Dan didn't judge on that matter. After all, he was going for a woman.

Rich hadn't fared well following their attack on the invaders who had killed Joe, and his nightmares recurred too often for him to be of any dependable use now. He wanted to stay in his cocoon where he cleaned the guns obsessively. Where he felt safe. Dan didn't blame him.

Mike spoke to Dan in private, eager to get his point across but not wanting to be seen to be in league with him by the others. Mike was loyal to Dan, as Dan had saved his life and that of his daughter,

Alice. She wanted to stay, and he could never leave her behind. Dan thanked Mike, told him that he understood and made him promise to look after the interests of the group.

After all, Dan had built it, and he didn't want it to fail.

Plans were being drawn up for their journey, and every spare minute was spent working out the logistics for such a risky venture.

The first problem was their personal equipment. Realistically, they would have to be carrying most of what they needed.

Vehicles. What should they take? Should they take things they could abandon on the south coast or try to find a way to get the vehicles to the continent?

"Much easier to find a boat that doesn't take vehicles," Mitch said, offering his opinion. "We could take a couple of scrambler bikes and use them to range out for appropriate vehicles."

That seemed a better option to Dan, who was worried that he would be seen to take the flagships of their fleet on what was being dubbed a suicide mission.

"OK," Dan said to his assembled planning party of Mitch, Leah, Neil and Marie. "Get ourselves to the south coast and find boats. Where?"

"Poole Harbour," said Neil with his eyes glazed over in memory. "Most sheltered place, and full of millionaires' yachts from what I remember."

"From there to France is only a few hours," Dan said, moving on.

"I've got another idea," said Mitch, leaning back and sipping his coffee. "Closest landing to Germany. From there, we scavenge whatever transport we can at the military camps. That's going to be the best bet for getting our hands on kit which can take us all the way."

Dan liked where this was heading. Proper military vehicles were likely the only things which could sway him from his love of Land Rovers. The selfish and childish pang at having to leave his Discovery behind stung him again; the car and the dog were part of his new identity.

"Amsterdam?" offered Marie, pointing her finger on the map. "It'll be a few more hours by boat, but the Channel should still be calm this time of year, shouldn't it? That's much closer to Germany than landing in Cherbourg or wherever."

"Right," said Dan as he tapped his pen on his pad, "get to Poole Harbour, get a boat big enough to take us to Amsterdam, a couple of days over country to Germany?" He looked at Mitch.

"Maybe a week. We have no idea about the lay of the land there, so we'd need to go carefully," Mitch answered.

"A week to the army camps, resupply and onwards," Dan said.

"Then how do we cross to Africa?" asked Leah.

Nobody had the solution.

She spun her map around and slid it to the centre of the table.

"Longer by land," she said. "Bulgaria, Turkey, Israel and over the Gulf via the Gaza Strip to Egypt."

At the mention of those countries, the mood fell considerably; many had been war-torn hells before it happened, so meeting any survivors there was likely to be a very dangerous occurrence.

"Or we cross the Alps, go straight down the boot of Italy and cross the Mediterranean somehow. That will land us with just a few thousand miles of Africa to get through."

Leah wasn't completely unaware that she had just offered an uncertain route as an alternative to a dangerous one, but there was no way to sugarcoat it.

Dan stood and stretched.

"OK, everyone. Have a think and we'll pick it up again tomorrow."

PROPER PREPARATION PREVENTS PISS-POOR PERFORMANCE

Mitch had self-designated as their official quartermaster, helped by Rich, who felt no shame in ensuring they were well equipped. Each person had been outfitted with the right clothing and a "Bergen," as he called it. To most people, this was an impossibly large backpack, but the Army's institutionalised language was impossible to eradicate. The two seemed to speak a whole new language at times to outsiders; talk of "tabbing" and "yomping" when everyone else would say "walking" created frequent confusion.

Firearms were sequestered and ammunition set aside. Each member of the party was carrying something lethal – even Pip, who was instructed in the use of a small nine-millimetre semi-automatic. They carried shotguns, three suppressed carbines, a few backup weapons, and one of the large Mk14 battle rifles.

Of the most important items issued were a can opener and a spork; wherever any of them were, they all had the ability to eat. They would have to find places along the way to loot for food and water, as well as wash their clothes as they went, as they couldn't carry too many spares.

When Dan went to medical to ask Kate for a comprehensive trauma kit, he was met by her and Sera. The door was shut after him and he was asked to sit down.

This felt too much like an intervention ambush for his liking, and he anticipated an appeal to his better sense to call off the expedition.

They sat opposite him and a short silence ensued. Dan was determined not to be swayed by any argument, so Sera's opening words left him open-mouthed and utterly lost for any answer.

"We're coming with you," she said bluntly.

Dan was dumbstruck, and his lack of answer seemed to anger Sera instantly. They had always been the same with each other: able to argue over anything.

"Oh no, really, you're most very welcome," she said mockingly. She opened her mouth to say more but Dan silenced her.

"Why?" he asked. "I thought you two were happy here."

Kate answered. "Because you need us. Marie needs us," she said simply. It seemed she would ever follow her calling to where she was most urgently required.

"And because I'm bored," said Sera. "I saw Pete's truck yesterday. It has a sticker on it saying 'one life – live it,' and I intend to. There's no point in surviving everything we've been through if we are just going to cower here and wait to die."

He looked at them both, and he thought he could see a hint of excitement in their eyes. They talked some more, and Dan brought them up to speed on where the plans were at. They both raised questioning eyebrows about the parts that relied on some random element of luck, but neither were swayed. He had his medical team.

"Lizzie and Alice will be fine dealing with this place. They've been as well trained as I can manage," said Kate.

With that, Dan rose uncertainly, almost dizzy at his good fortune.

The following day, Dan and Leah took Mitch and Jimmy out to find the scouting motorbikes they discussed. Curiously, the only motorbikes they had encountered since it happened were now synonymous with the more unpleasant of survivors. Even hearing a motorbike engine sparked some small element of primeval fear in more than a few of them.

Leah drove the big 4x4 back with Ash sitting beside her, swarmed like tiny satellites by the three men buzzing around her on their newly acquired 250cc dirt bikes. All brand-new Hondas liberated from a motorcycle dealership nearby and with barely any miles on them, Neil was eager to get them to his workshop and prepare them.

He had plans to remove every reflective surface and paint them matt black. Mitch joked that he should add weapon mounts, which Neil didn't take as a joke.

Endless plans were made, equipment was piled up and those intending to leave gave away possessions that couldn't be taken with them. One by one, the people planning to leave found themselves segregated, eating separately, as though the intention to abandon the prison was contagious.

THE TIME HAS COME

When the expedition prepared to leave in order to make the crossing before the weather turned, the atmosphere was one of obvious disapproval. Even anger. Most members of the group were tight-lipped about their opinions, but it was obvious that there was no coming back from this.

Steve agreed to assist in dropping an advance party off at the harbour to find and prepare the necessary boat or boats for their journey. This was intended to save them a few days of waiting, as they were eager to get the crossing over with while the seas were at their calmest.

With a small sense of ceremony, Dan took one last lap of the Ops room before laying the keys to their flagship – his impressively equipped Discovery – on the table. His fingers lingered on the keys for a second before he turned and left.

The huge helicopter surged upwards with Mitch and Adam on board going ahead with minimal supplies and a promise of finding a boat for their arrival. A small convoy set off from the prison shortly afterwards. Steve's old Defender, the very first vehicle Dan and Neil had scavenged all that time ago, went up front packed with as many bags and boxes as could be wedged in or tied on top. Following them were another two of the older vehicles to be abandoned in the south, and one of the small lorries carrying all the spare equipment, motorbikes and stores.

No grand farewell. No celebrations or well wishing, just a cold goodbye and the firm belief that none of them would ever be seen again.

The surprise additions to the party were Phil – their airsick mechanic deserter from Richards's unhappy camp – and Emma. She had always assumed that she was going but had forgotten to actually mention this fact to anyone until a few days before when she naively asked what she should pack.

Sixteen of them – seventeen if counting the excited dog jumping over people in the lead vehicle – left at a sedate pace. They drove up the long, picturesque approach, out of the main road emerging through the encroaching trees, turned left and headed for the motorway. They were travelling in sufficient force so as not to worry about being overpowered, but certain pairs of eyes were always alert.

They made good ground that day, stopping only twice for a break where Dan and Leah fanned out in defence by autonomous action. In the afternoon, someone called out that they could see Steve flying back in the distance.

Dan called a halt at sundown and cleared a small building where people grabbed a spot to sleep. A noise from the back of the lorry made those who heard it freeze. Dan drew his sidearm, nodded to Leah, who took a knee and aimed her carbine, and then threw open the vertical shutter.

Henry stood bathed in sudden light, embarrassed at being caught. Dan's shouting could be heard by everyone as he tore into the teenage boy. He had been told that he wasn't coming due to his age and the fact that he would need protecting. His counterarguments that he was older than Leah fell away into silence as she rounded on him and stared him down. He was big and fit, but very immature.

Marie took Dan aside and convinced him that he should allow him to stay, primarily because they couldn't afford the time to return him.

Dan agreed grudgingly, but had one final piece of advice for the boy. "If you put anyone in danger, you're on your bloody own. Am I understood?" he growled at him, nose to nose.

Henry's fear was palpable, but he solemnly promised to not get in the way.

It was settled. They were going, and none of them knew if they were ever coming back.

HARD LANDING

Steve's fear grew in intensity as each jolt or shudder of the ailing aircraft fed back through his limbs. He was fearful that he would drop from the sky at any point, but was still just a little too far from home to abandon the helicopter where he was.

If he could only nurse it back, then maybe it could be fixed. In truth, it was his own stubbornness which led to disaster; if only he had finally accepted that this, as unenjoyable as it was, would be his last flight, then he could have landed safely and made it home by nightfall.

He didn't. Maybe being on his own was a bad thing, because the presence of another life would have made him less cavalier about the dangers and infinitely more responsible.

The struggling helicopter surged over the treetops near the prison, desperately low as he fought to control the rear of the bird. The intermittent failure of the oil pressure somewhere thirty feet behind him was causing the tail rotor to lose power, threatening to spin over ten tonnes of screaming metal into the unforgiving ground.

As the house came into sight, Steve lost control of his aircraft.

If only he had not tried to nurse it all the way home, if he had just stopped a few miles short, then he could have got it on the ground in one piece and walked away.

As it was, Chris was on the farm when he heard the tortured noise of dying machinery and looked up at the skyline. He had a front-row seat as the Merlin crashed through the trees and spun to the ground, destroying one of the solar-panel towers as it came down.

Steve, despite controlling a crippled thing, did well and kept it level on impact.

The belly of the helicopter slammed into the ground and ploughed great furrows as the resistance of the earth held it tight. The dying rotors continued to spin as they decelerated, digging cruel gouges into the soft turf.

Chris stood useless and open-mouthed at the horror he had witnessed. His wits returned to him, and he ran headlong through the field from the farm towards the wreckage.

BOATS

"Do you know anything about boats?" asked Mitch pensively of Adam as they walked among the rooms of a lavish seafront house.

Adam stopped. "No," he said. "You?"

"Some. Not much, really," Mitch answered, before they both laughed.

They had spent hours looking for a good place to set up for a couple of days until the convoy reached them. They found the issue of boats to be easier than expected, as almost all of the extravagant houses had their own crafts on their private moorings. The keys all had bright, floating keyrings attached to them. Of the first few, two were so small that they would need both to get just the people over the water and a third for their minimal equipment. Another had taken on water and sat shimmering just under the water level.

They had waited in cover after their loud drop-off, both ready with rifles after Adam's crash course in military weapon discipline. Mitch had been quick and thorough in his instruction, which was sensible, seeing as he was training his own backup.

Nobody seemed to have noticed their arrival, and after an hour, Mitch called for them to break cover and start their search. The sun drew low and they settled in, eating cold beans and rice pudding from the can and enjoying a companionable drink as they talked.

They rose with the morning sun and continued their search.

By midday, they found what they were dreaming of: a three-decked yacht on the far side of the bay. It took them nearly an hour to row a small boat over and another two to find the keys. They put their supplies on board and cleared out all detritus which they didn't need. The boat was wonderful and modern, every bit as plush and luxurious as the houses they searched. The controls weren't dissimilar to those of a car, and without too much difficulty it was piloted over to the opposite side of the bay where – with some contact with the jetty – it was moored successfully.

"It's called parking by braille, son!" yelled Mitch cheerfully as Adam winced at the contact between fibreglass and wood.

They settled in to rest for the day, planning to source more fuel the following day for the journey when, hopefully, the rest of the party would join them.

DUE SOUTH

Two days of hard travelling had brought them into Dorset. Leah, with her keen senses, was the first to claim she could smell the sea air.

They had encountered nobody on their journey, much to Dan's relief. Even though most of their party was armed, he knew all too well that only a few of them had ever fired a shot in anger or been faced with the terrifying prospect and sound of incoming rounds.

Tired and travel-weary from their ponderous haul, they drove down to the seafront and set up a defence. As agreed, the horn on the Land Rover was sounded three long times.

They waited.

Mitch, for all his simplicities, had a sense for the theatrical. Just as Dan was beginning to lose his composure and organise a search, movement showed on the water. Dan barely contained his excitement as the grandest yacht he had ever laid eyes on cruised into sight.

The three horn blasts were returned, and a waving Adam was visible on the bow. He held aloft his weapon in celebration, and Dan was struck by the sudden beauty of the setting. A silhouetted boat with an armed man standing tall on the foredeck filled his heart with hope and a lust for further excitement.

Mitch brought the boat into mooring as Adam leapt down and tied the hull to the jetty. Members of the group ran to them, and Dan fought down the urge to call them back. He needed that excitement to run deep for this whole wild goose chase to work.

Mitch stepped down smartly and cracked off a crisp salute to Dan. He adopted Neil's signature style and returned the pose as the others climbed aboard making noises similar to those of small children running into a play barn.

The comedy salutes cracked into huge smiles and the gestures evolved into a firm handshake as the two friends congratulated each other without words.

"It's a three-deck Sunseeker," Mitch said impressively, hiding his total ignorance by repeating the facts he read on the deck. "Should fit us all in fine," he continued as he strolled along the jetty like he was trying to sell it. "The GPS is useless, obviously, but the fuel gauge is showing half-full. We'll need to rectify that when we can find where they keep the boat petrol or whatever it takes. Let me show you the best bit!"

Mitch smiled and walked towards the rear of the boat before turning and gesturing at the flat stern.

Dan felt his heart skip a little as he read the ornate scroll in big lettering across the back of the yacht.

Hope.

MAN DOWN

Chris sprinted desperately over the uneven ground, stumbling as he ran. Others were starting to pour from the house now as the brutal and cacophonous sound interrupted their day.

The rotor blades had stopped turning by the time Chris reached the wreckage – not that he noticed as he threw himself towards the side door and fought to open it. All around him were the tortured noises of the stalled engines, hissing and screeching into his brain.

His panic made him clumsy, but he managed to force open the door and climb inside. Fuel poured from the ruptured spare tank to his left, spraying him with the strange-smelling oily substance, but he didn't notice at the time. He pulled himself through the aperture to the cockpit and found Steve slumped into the harness, unconscious. The seat had collapsed on impact, as it was designed to do to prevent serious injury, but as Steve wasn't wearing a protective helmet, his head had suffered a terrible blow. His scalp was covered in blood, and it continued to pour down his face to run into his lap.

"STEVE," bawled Chris over and over, getting no response. It suddenly occurred to him that the fuel may catch on fire and that they could both go up in a fireball. He moved Steve's head aside, adding his blood to the fuel covering his own body, and fought with the harness to try and release him.

His hands were sticky from the slick fluids, making the task almost impossible under such stress, but he finally managed to gain enough purchase on the latch to turn it and free his friend.

As he did, Steve's deadweight fell towards him due to the uneven angle at which the broken aircraft lay. Both men fell backwards into the right-hand seat, and Chris struggled to regain his footing. He heard screams and shouts from outside, but the primitive fear of fire cut through his terror to shout at them to stay away.

He half-dragged, half-carried Steve to the doorway, where they both fell out onto the ruined turf. He lay there for a second before the thoughts of a super-heated explosion came to him again.

"GET BACK," he screamed, making half of the assembled onlookers turn and run as they too realised the possibility of the imminent explosion. Chris regained his footing and dragged Steve clear, ever fearful that they would be engulfed in flames at any second.

Others ran to him to help Chris up, and Kev let out a bellow of terrified rage and picked Steve up bodily before running back to the house, carrying him like a child, his lifeless limbs hanging and bouncing grotesquely.

All around Chris, people were breaking down in tears. The sobs cut through his fogged brain and brought him back to the present. He looked up at the face in front of him as the repeated questions became intelligible.

"Are you OK? What happened?" asked Jay, wild-eyed in front of him.

For a second, Chris thought it was Dan who stood in front of him, tall and dark-haired. "Bastard," he said, shaking. "It's your fucking fault."

Jay was visibly taken back but put the response down to shock. How was it his fault?

Chris sat where he was, shaking from the effort and the adrenaline surging through his body. "Bastard," he said again.

Kev still howled like a wounded animal as he ran the short distance to the house. He burst through the main doors like a battering ram and straight into medical.

He threw Steve onto the bed, startling Lizzie and Alice even though they had heard the crash. He bellowed again, dancing on the spot and pointing at Steve. His bellow turned into a strange, high-pitched keening noise as tears flowed down his face. He turned to face the wall and maintained his pained noises.

Jimmy wasn't there to calm him down, and he stayed in that toddler state until Maggie came in to soothe him. She gently led him away as Lizzie and Alice were feverishly working to the best of their abilities to stem the flow of blood pouring from Steve's head.

"There's so much blood!" said Alice as the panic started to affect her. Painful memories of her own father bleeding so profusely cut through to her, distracting her from the task.

"I can't find where it's coming from," said Lizzie, calm and focused. "Cut his clothes off," she instructed the younger woman, taking her attention away from the free-flowing blood.

Alice started at his ankles, cutting up the legs of his flight suit with heavy medical shears and exposing bare skin as she went. She gasped when she uncovered his right leg, standing back to press a bloody hand to her mouth in shock.

Lizzie stopped what she was doing to look at the source of her shock and saw that Steve's lower right leg was clearly broken and discoloured by livid bruising.

"Focus," Lizzie snapped. "The leg can wait, but the bleeding won't," she said, before returning to the task of mopping away the pouring blood to try and locate the source on his skull.

Alice stepped back, having cut away the suit to expose his broken body; bruises covered him everywhere, including the blackening circle over the left side of his ribcage. Lizzie glanced at that, worried about possible organ damage and internal bleeding. She forced herself to concentrate: internal bleeding second, stop the blood flow from his head first.

"BP cuff and oxygen SATS," she said to Alice, who ran to get the equipment to monitor his vital signs.

"Gotcha, you bastard," Lizzie said with an angry glee as she finally located the deep gash high over Steve's right ear exposing the white of his skull. She put pressure on the wound and wrapped a dressing on tightly. "Hold this," she snapped at Alice, who did as she was told and went to keep the pressure on the head wound. "Cuts to the head bleed like crazy," Lizzie said reassuringly, as much to herself as Alice. "They always look worse than they are."

She worked feverishly, checking Steve's vitals before starting a top-to-toe survey starting with shining a torch in his eyes to see if his pupils reacted. Luckily they did, but the rest did not look good.

Deep gash to the head, broken ribs, badly broken leg. Those were the obvious injuries anyway; he likely had internal bleeding and some damage to his organs from the impact to his torso, and that leg would cause no end of trouble if she couldn't set it soon. She stood back and looked at him again, deep in thought.

"I'm going to have to set the leg while he's out. It's better that way," she said, hoping she was right.

She strode to the door and pulled it open, finding a bewildered crowd of concerned men and women in front of her. "Mark, Paul," she said, beckoning them inside and shutting the door again, "I need you to help me. I need one of you to hold his upper leg while we pull the lower part down to set the bone."

Paul nodded gravely while Mark looked sick. He had spent enough time in this room being treated, the testimony to that being the thick scars all over his body from when he was attacked by a pack of dogs on a scavenging run.

They got into position while Alice continued to check him over. She spoke softly to him, so softly that none of them heard her words. She was soothing him, telling him it would be OK, speaking as much to herself as to him.

Paul held on tight to Steve's thigh just above the knee, and Mark held the ankle. Lizzie looked them both in the eye, bent to take purchase just below the break, and steadied herself.

"Now," she said. All three began to pull, but it wasn't enough. "Harder!" she grunted, feeling the jagged edges of the bones grate against each other. They were red-faced and breathing heavily at the effort, struggling to force the contracted and ruptured muscles of his leg to give enough to return it to a semblance of its original shape. Eventually, centimetre by sickening centimetre, the leg stretched until a final crunching sound indicated that they had succeeded.

"Alice. Splint," she said, breathless. She didn't dare let go of the twisted limb in case it returned to its former unnatural shape. They strapped his leg tight in an inflatable boot before relaxing again.

Mark ran from the room, unable to keep himself from fountaining vomit from his mouth as he went.

Paul smiled nervously, hoping that they had done well, but Lizzie just stared at Steve. He hadn't made a sound throughout what would have probably been the most painful experience of his life.

"Thank you, Paul," she said quietly, not taking her eyes from the battered and bloody man on the bed.

Paul left, and the two women stood in silence.

Lizzie picked up a sharp implement, jabbing it harshly into the sole of Steve's good foot. No response. Not even a twitch.

Dismayed, she hung her head.

MOTION LOTION PART II

"Boat petrol?" asked Dan, amused at Mitch's blatant ignorance.

"Yeah! What else does it run on? Fairy dust and unicorn farts?"

Both men laughed as they walked away from the residential side of the harbour towards the commercial buildings in the distance. Ash loped alongside, eagerly sniffing the new smells of the seaside.

The whole group had spent a comfortable and happy night in one of the seafront mansions. Furniture and beds were claimed by adults acting like children at a sleepover. Marie strode in, playing the part of the matriarch and loudly expelling an excited gaggle of people from the master bedroom before laying claim to it for her and Dan.

"Pregnant woman coming through!" she announced, instantly regretting her words as she saw Ana out of the corner of her eye.

Mitch and Adam hadn't located a fuel source on the day of their arrival, and the matter was becoming time-sensitive.

"We need a full tank at least. Neil reckons the fuel tank is as big as his old trailer tanker and that was five thousand litres. Maybe fifteen hours' worth of driving," said Dan, relaxed but still alert as they walked.

"Sailing," corrected Mitch, happily displaying that he had at least some knowledge of nautical matters.

"Sailing, then," repeated Dan, "but that should still get us to where we're going easily enough."

"What's the plan for finding where we're going?" Mitch asked, genuinely curious.

"Straight over to France heading south, turn left and follow the coastline until we think we're there," said Dan, accepting that he didn't really know but still unable to admit the fact to anyone. "If we go for about eight hours, then we'd have to be about right, I reckon. We've got maps of the continent, so we should be able to recognise the landmarks or something."

"Well, we won't be going anywhere unless we find more diesel," Mitch said peevishly at having been corrected.

They walked for almost forty minutes, not wanting to take a vehicle for the noise it would make and also to save what fuel they had to be siphoned off to add to the tank of the *Hope* and further their range. They would also struggle to get a vehicle down to the edge of the water in most places, so they were happy to do the reconnaissance on foot and aimed to bring the boat to the source.

A smell drifted through the air to them, gone as soon as it was detected.

Both men froze. Both were well attuned to the dangers and had been in countless situations where a lapse in concentration or an ignored sense could spell death.

Silently and without instruction, both men readied their weapons and dropped to a crouch in the shadows of the building line. Dan turned to Mitch, knowing that he too had sensed the presence of another person.

The smell was unmistakably that of something cooking, more specifically a barbecue. A glance at the huge dog confirmed that there was indeed something edible within a mile, as his snout was raised and

41

his ears pricked. Dan thought that if that dog had an Achilles heel, it was his stomach.

The pair crept forward quietly, not sacrificing speed for silence but being careful to avoid any sound which could give away their presence. Slowly, they made their way onwards, picking up the smell every so often. After a short time, it was constant – definitely a barbecue. Dan fancied that he heard a voice, as fleeting as the smell had come to them at first, and gone just as quickly.

The sun had dropped behind the buildings by then, shadowing them slightly, but they were still horribly exposed, two armed men in black clothing creeping along a deserted promenade with a grey wolf skulking along with them. There were slightly more conspicuous ways to be viewed, but short of riding in on a tank, they would hardly seem friendly to any watchful eyes.

They crept along, under cover of a shoulder-high wall, as the sounds of talking and laughter were close. Eye contact between the two men gave mutual reassurance that both knew they were close, confirmed by the smallest of growls from the throat of Ash.

Two ways to play this, thought Dan: sneak past and stay hidden, or come out and talk.

He mulled it over, getting a prod in the back from Mitch. He mimed speaking with his hand and shrugged his shoulders, suggesting that they be overt. Dan looked down, thinking. He looked back at his friend and nodded.

The two men rose up and walked carelessly, talking about nothing as they went and sounding for the benefit of anyone close enough to hear them like they didn't have a care in the world.

Their plan worked in that they didn't startle them. Their aimless chatting provoked instant silence from up ahead, followed by shouts and then more silence.

"Hello?" called Dan.

Three men appeared on the higher ground to their left just up ahead. Two were armed, although with nothing which would pose any real danger to their automatic weapons. Ash adopted a protective stance in front of his master and bared his teeth with a snarl.

"Play nice," muttered Dan to silence the animal as he raised a hand and strode forward.

CRISIS COUNCIL

Lexi felt the mood in the room to be a little too cold for her liking. She sat in relative silence following Dan's advice from long ago to hold your tongue until you had something important to say; the very fact that she was even thinking about him right then and there would likely have sent some of the others present into a tailspin.

"OK, everyone!" Mike said, raising his voice to cut through the multitude of competing voices.

Silence eventually reigned in the room, allowing the engineer a brief respite from his headache and a small chance to regroup.

"OK," he said again, quieter this time, "we have all agreed that I take Head of House on an interim basis and amalgamate Engineering under the same roof. Andrew?"

The smaller man at the table, permanently wearing a look of fear, raised his eyes to meet Mike's.

"You will take over Logistics along with Supplies, as the two are obviously closely linked. Lizzie will remain as Head of Medical, Cara in Catering and Chris for the Farms."

He looked at his folded hands on the table before raising his eyes to the blonde woman dressed in black.

"And Lexi will remain on the council as the acting Head of Operations until such time as Steve regains his health."

Lizzie cleared her throat, but a warning glance from Mike made her keep the thought hidden for now.

Lexi nodded slowly, aware of the gravity of the task laid at her feet but not fully understanding how it would affect her yet: the sleepless nights, the additional duties, the stress of training replacement Rangers when all of the bravest men and women had left them.

She cleared her own throat, stopped toying with the chunky Land Rover keys clipped to her vest and sat up straight. "I need to select at least two of our group and train them in the basics of being a Ranger. Rich will be able to help, but he's too fragile still to be of any use on a mission. As it stands, I'm our only gun now, and we need more."

She tried to emulate Dan's easy authority. She had always marvelled at his ability to command people around him, to gain instant cooperation and obedience, not from fear but from respect for his abilities and their belief in him. She knew her own words were a far cry from the inspirational things she had heard come from him since Dan had first stridden in to where they were cowering, fussing around a man so mortally injured that he was effectively already dead.

From that moment, she had idolised Dan and would have followed him anywhere. She had even thought she loved him for a time. Her thoughts drifted off to him. To Marie. To Leah and Neil. To all the people she vowed never to abandon, to lay down her own life for theirs.

Now she wished she had tried harder to convince Paul to leave with them, but her love for him blinded her to the truth.

Without Dan and Marie to hold this place together, they were weak.

Steve's catastrophic helicopter crash had just been the beginning; everything was starting to come apart. People were arguing and fighting back against the instructions of those in charge of the different areas for little or no reason. Everyone seemed to want to express some form of anger, and it was threatening to tear their whole society apart. Everywhere she looked, there was upset and discord, conflict and resistance. Lexi felt that the biggest part of her job now was to keep internal discipline tight.

As the shrunken council disintegrated to their own thoughts and hiding places, her mind spun from thought to thought. She finally rested on the notion that to maintain order, she must recruit someone capable enough to ensure that tempers were kept in check. She stopped playing with the keys to her new Discovery and went to find Paul.

Lizzie stood over Steve's supine form, nervously picking at her lips as she brooded. He was breathing fine by himself, of that there was no doubt, and as far as she could tell he had no serious brain injury, or his pupils would have been unevenly dilated at the very least. They were reactive to light, which was a good sign, but he was still out cold.

No pain response. His right leg was a mess. His torso was battered, but luckily the bruising hadn't spread too much, so the internal bleeding hopefully wasn't as bad as she had feared. Other than that, all she could do was pump him full of fluids and antibiotics and pray.

The catheter she had placed in him was producing a steady supply of bloody urine, to be expected after the major trauma of the crash, and all that remained now was to watch and wait. And hope that he lived.

Alice had taken turns with her to sleep in one of the unoccupied beds in medical as the other kept watch over him. It seemed to Lizzie that they had lost only a few of their number, but she couldn't help but feel that the best of them had gone away and those that remained were the weakest links of a longer chain. She wished now that she had summoned the courage to go, to encourage them all to abandon their sanctuary and follow the wild goose chase to its uncertain conclusion in far-off Africa.

No turning back now. There was no way she could stray further from Steve than the dining hall for now, and those kinds of responsibilities weighed heavy on a person's selfish thoughts of escapism and adventure. With a sigh, she pulled up a chair and a book to pass the time as she monitored the vital signs flashing on the monitor while her only medical backup slept soundly.

MEXICAN STANDOFF

"Greetings!" said one of the men cheerfully, holding a shotgun.

While his tone was genial, the demeanour of the others was anything but; weapons were raised at them and more bodies appeared on the higher ground and threatened to overshadow their position.

Militarily speaking, Dan and Mitch were properly flanked. Definitely time to seek a diplomatic solution.

While they were outnumbered and trapped on lower ground, Dan's keen eye noted that the three shotguns he could now see were a poor match for their two automatic weapons. He knew that Mitch would have known this too, so felt comfortable enough to try diplomacy in the knowledge that two trained men with superior firepower and experience, combined with a very intimidating dog, could not be in too much danger from these men with comparatively rudimentary weapons to their own.

The educated assumption of superiority, in the firepower stakes at least, made for a more comfortable bargaining position.

"Hi," Dan said, surreptitiously lowering his carbine and letting it hang on the sling. He put a hand down ready to grab Ash's rig in case he decided to go for one of the men facing them.

The man handed his weapon to a squat sidekick and jumped down from the wall to stand at their level, effectively putting himself in the kill zone of any ambush and nullifying any advantage they had over the two outsiders.

Up close, he was a big man, dark-skinned and heavyset, standing well over six feet. His physical presence was made less intimidating by his genuine smile; he beamed at them like he was greeting a pair of old friends as he extended a huge hand. Dan accepted the offer, felt his own hand engulfed by the man, and squeezed tightly.

His obvious excitement at meeting others was not jaded by the weapons they carried; in fact, the man seemed not to notice at all.

"Simon," he boomed as he continued to shake Dan's hand rigorously.

Dan responded with his own name, nodding to his companion and introducing Mitch. Simon turned the full power of his handshake to Mitch, who Dan saw wince a little at the pressure.

Out of the corner of his eye, Dan noticed that the others didn't seem so trusting. Some visibly relaxed, lowering their weapons and smiling too, but one man stood out. He kept his shotgun pointed at the three men and wore a look of such misery on his face that Dan suspected he would pull the trigger given even the slightest hint of provocation.

Dan was slightly disarmed by the overt elation that the big man showed, and up close he saw that he bore a small resemblance to a famous singer from years back. The thought drifted away as he wondered if he were still out there somewhere, and if anyone was looking for him. He snapped his senses back to the present, and possibly dangerous, situation.

"Gentlemen," said Simon, still smiling widely, "how can we help you?"

"Diesel," said Mitch. "We're after diesel for our boat."

"Boat?" Simon repeated with genuine interest. "Where are you going?" He switched his glance between the two men, sensing the obvious secrecy in their mannerisms before Dan interjected.

"Look," he said, deciding on honesty, "we've had a rough time of it and haven't met too many friendlies since it happened. We mean no disrespect."

Simon seemed affronted, hurt even, that someone would think him unkind to others. His own attitude towards them appeared to have transferred to his whole group, as they relaxed. Simon profusely declared their intentions to be honest, swearing on his life that he meant them no harm. He invited them to join him for the most British of icebreakers: tea.

Their appearance in this small camp had started as trespassers and suddenly evolved into the status of honoured guests as they were ushered up the steps and into a building which appeared to have become the temporary headquarters of Simon's happy band.

Happy with the exception of the short, sour-faced man who still glared at them like he was yearning for the excuse to put them down. He eyed their equipment with evident jealousy and made no attempt to hide his scorn.

Ash had relaxed visibly, especially after some bits of food were sent his way. The only exception being the wary eye he kept on the man glaring at them. Like all dog owners, Dan thought that if Ash didn't like someone, then he probably wouldn't.

"Down, Riley," Simon admonished him. "Good boy," he said, prompting laughs from the others at the short man's expense.

Riley did not look impressed, and forced a short-muttered conversation on Simon, making him bend down to hear the low whispers.

As the taller man listened, his eyes glazed over in a sudden, furious anger. It quickly evaporated, but Dan had seen it. This man was no fool, no matter how many people mistook his kindness for weakness.

Ash did not like the tone of the conversation and let out another low, menacing growl until Dan calmed him.

Whatever Simon muttered back was not to Riley's liking, and he stalked away with a cold look of anger evident on his face to loiter at the fringes of the assembled group. Simon straightened himself and returned to the genial soul who just seemed to want to speak to someone new.

"Thank you, Riley," he said sarcastically over his shoulder. "Don't mind him," he said in a quieter voice, making light of the power struggle they had just witnessed. "He managed to bully and threaten his way to some position of power among the others and now thinks he knows better than me. Back-stabbing little shit." Simon's smile did little to remove the power of his words, and Dan marked the angry little man as one to avoid.

Water was boiled, eager listeners gathered, and brews were poured. There appeared to be about ten of them – all men – gathered in the building, and they clearly hadn't been there long.

Simon laid out the highlights of their story, not too dissimilar to Dan's own, and told them how he was the proud leader of what they called their "colony". Mostly farmers, and those who weren't were being taught how to be, they had sent out people to search further afield for supplies to keep them growing.

Dan responded with their own story, leaving out such details as the eradication of Slaver's Bay, as it had become known, and the annihilation of the Welsh invaders. He did recount how they had been attacked and had successfully repelled the assault, which raised eyebrows among the gathering and not less than a few noises of admiration.

"Two peas in a pod, we are!" boomed Simon happily. "We just want what's best for our own." He raised his cup in a gesture of companionship and solidarity, which Dan mirrored.

Time to get to the point.

"So, what brings you all here, then?" Dan asked politely. "Big party for a supply run."

The mood went colder as soon as he had spoken; clearly a raw nerve had been touched by his words.

"Same as you," said Simon quietly, sipping his drink and staring into the small flames radiating from the camp cooker used to boil the water. "Fuel. There's thousands of gallons of the stuff in a boatyard not far from here. We sent a lad last week, and when he didn't come back, a couple of the boys went to look for him."

He went quiet, saddened by the story he was recounting. He took another sip of his drink in silence. A quick glance around the assembled faces showed them all deep in thought, eyes cast to the floor.

"And you didn't find him?" asked Mitch.

"Oh, we found him all right," said their host angrily, "we found him."

It seemed that Simon would tell them nothing more when another of the men spoke up. "They hanged him," he said angrily. "They fucking strung him up and left him there with a sign on him: Looter." He said no more, simply turned away from the group and walked off a distance.

Simon picked up the story. "The lads we sent to look for him found him like that. John there was his cousin," he said simply to excuse the manners of the man who had left them to talk.

"Who?" asked Dan, the familiar feelings of anger rising once again at the injustice of murder.

"There's a group who've taken over the docks, controlling the whole boatyard. It's further down the coast, and when we went there, we had to run away. They've got rifles."

The simple facts as they were laid out were a pure problem-meets-solution matter for Dan; the group ensconced at the docks had what they needed and were defending it. The only options were to seek a different solution or to use force. The decision to use force was based solely on a risk basis.

Any risk of loss was too great to consider for Dan's small group, but his pathological sense of justice, of righting wrongs, ran deep. He wanted to help, but he could see no way of doing that without risking the lives of his group. He was torn between helping Simon's band and getting what they needed for themselves straight away, or leaving the others to their own devices and finding another solution.

Mitch spoke as he was thinking, asking the relevant questions about numbers, weapons, vantage points, access and egress. None of the group could answer these basics, and it became clear that while committed and well-meaning, not one of them was a trained man. These men were a farmers militia and not soldiers.

Dan forced the thought of helping them away; as likeable as the man in front of them was, Dan's own group would have to be the ones to do the wet work if this went down.

He couldn't take that risk.

"There's got to be an alternative elsewhere," he suggested to Simon. "Better to shop around than get into a fight over it, surely?"

Simon thought about it for a while, seemingly considering Dan's words, but truly he already knew that they could not hope to attack the other group. It was a matter of petty revenge, and that wasn't worth the lives of more good people.

"Perhaps you're right," Simon said finally, "but with your help, we could do it."

Dan knew this was coming, and he was conscious not to let his true feelings pour out and cause offence. He explained that they were going to a specific place and needed to set off as soon as they could. They couldn't afford to expend the ammunition, or to put their few soldiers at risk.

"I'm sorry," Dan finished lamely. "If we could help, we would. I'll speak to the others tonight and see if we can find some other way we can help each other."

Simon accepted this gracefully. He knew that to ask strangers to put their lives at risk to help him was unlikely to yield success, but he had tried to ask as gently as possible. He was about to say more when Riley stood and spoke.

"Typical," he snarled, "they may look the part but they're just as weak as you are." Riley's gaze lingered on Simon before he turned abruptly and stomped away. "Pathetic," he said, spitting over his shoulder as he left the room.

HOUSE OF CARDS

Lexi barely left the site for the next two days. She had to break up two fights between residents, and on one occasion needed the newly black-clad Paul to lay one of the men out cold by taking him down in a neck hold until he lost consciousness. To say that tempers were high was a ridiculous understatement.

Divisions formed at mealtimes and a few people were vocal in claiming that the whole place would fall apart without Dan and the others who had left. It was an unhappy place with everyone deeply shocked by the helicopter crash.

The old Merlin wasn't just transport: it was a symbol. It was a mechanical demonstration that they were superior. That they were infallible.

When it smashed into the earth not two hundred metres from their home, that symbolism was shattered, and the people were left rocked and feeling vulnerable. That vulnerability became fear, and the fear became aggression.

People spoke of leaving. Others sat quietly and tried to hide their fear.

The council met again after the evening meal on the second night after the crash. Lexi gave her report about the internal discipline matters, expressing her concerns that she could not leave the site for fear that people would tear each other apart. Paul had been of some obvious help in keeping the peace, but his move into Ops was an interim solution at best.

They were vulnerable. The power vacuum that had been caused by so many of their key members leaving and taking their precious skills and knowledge with them had not even begun to be filled.

DEMOCRACY

"Head sheds meeting," Mitch called loudly to their group as they walked back in during the afternoon.

Head sheds was a military term he used for a decision-making meeting involving the key players of any group. Rank did not necessarily mean that obedience was expected. Everyone who had a point could make it, and the group would decide the best course of action.

The expected faces gathered: Dan, Marie, Mitch, Neil, Kate, Sera and Leah. Others who joined at the fringes were Adam, never far from Mitch now, and Pip. Her addition was unexpected, but she was welcome. Even Ash nosed his way into the circle, but not to offer any wisdom. He was there for the chance of food.

Dan relayed the details of their meeting with Simon, explaining that they had tried to make their excuses and leave but had been asked outright for help.

"They're farmers with shotguns," said Mitch, feeling the injustice at their persecution.

"It's not about two other groups pissing over territory," Dan said, not entirely believing it but not wanting to jeopardise the safety of the group over his need to fight bullies. "It's about the fuel. They have it and we need it, so we either fight them for it or we look elsewhere."

Silence reigned among the small huddle.

"Thoughts," Dan invited, familiar to some of the assembled, as he always wanted to hear other people's ideas.

Neil was the first to speak. "Look elsewhere. It may be the nearest and the best, but we could scavenge using hand pumps and the big tank on the Land Rover. It'll take us longer, but we can manage."

"It'll take too long," answered Mitch. "They have all the fuel we need and we can get it in one go."

Dan knew that the soldier really wanted to mix it with the group and see if they could handle a fighter instead of a farmer, reckoning that he would be far harder to kill. It was a prideful form of arrogance that they could ill afford, but one that Dan had been guilty of in the past on more than one occasion.

"Look elsewhere," said Kate, ever eager to avoid any bloodshed.

Sera nodded her agreement, as Dan thought she would.

He looked to the next face in the circle.

"Take it. They deserve what they get," said Adam, echoing Mitch.

Dan looked to Pip, who felt that they shouldn't pick a fight unless they had to. He looked to Ash, who returned his gaze with a daft expression and a lip tucked behind some teeth. That was his *I'm a good boy* face.

He chuckled and turned to Leah.

"Pros and cons," she said, full of competent confidence. "It's a one-hit shopping trip, and I agree that they deserve a bullet for killing unarmed survivors…"

"But?" Dan asked, knowing there was more.

"But we can't run the risk of losing anyone. There are few of us who know how to use a gun properly as it is; if even one of us gets hurt, then the whole trip could be ruined."

Nobody could argue with that, and Dan turned to the last person present.

"I agree with Leah," said Marie. "If things were different, then we would stay and help, but we can't. I'm sure I'm not the only one who thinks that it's already getting colder, and I don't want to be crossing the ocean when the weather is bad. We need to find an alternative. This time."

The decision was made by the group. As much as it pained him, he had to deny his help to a man he had liked. Simon's group would have to fend for themselves.

Small parties were detailed to go out and find as much fuel as they could the following morning, and they settled in for another evening. As the sun was fully down, so too the temperature dropped. As Dan stood on the grand balcony of their borrowed home to smoke, he looked out over the beautiful calm waters. Without light pollution, the surroundings were utterly stunning. Breathtaking.

The calm silence was shattered as his ears detected the unmistakable sounds of gunfire in the distance. He could make out an echoing, booming report of a shotgun followed by the more staccato sharp note of a rifle as the sounds echoed around the bay. He threw down his cigarette and strode back inside, snatching up his carbine as he moved.

"Leah. Mitch. With me," he said with purpose.

The two jumped up and quickly prepared for whatever would come next.

"Neil. Adam," he shouted. When they appeared, he told them to secure the house. "Lock it down and don't come out until we're back, and keep Ash inside. Jimmy?" He looked at the assembled faces.

"Here," came the reply.

"Keep watch on the front."

Jimmy nodded and hefted his shotgun.

Dan pulled back the bolt on his carbine and checked that he could see brass before striding purposefully through the expensive glass doorway and out into the night.

The three moved quickly and silently between the shadows, always one covering as the others moved. They flowed intrinsically, fluidly, playing out a story of endless hours of practice and years of experience. They leapfrogged like this for over a mile without the need for communication when the sounds of the gun battle faded to nothing.

As they approached the building line short of where Dan and Mitch had encountered the other group earlier, Leah gave a short, low whistle and took cover. The two men mimicked her, melting into the shadows to present smaller targets to whatever had spooked their young comrade.

Slowly, from the gloom, two men emerged. One was being supported by a bigger man and was pressing his hand to his left side. Sobs could be heard from the wounded man as he was almost dragged along the seafront away from the danger.

As the shapes became more recognisable, Dan saw that the big man was Simon. He broke cover and ran forwards, taking over the burden from the exhausted man. He hurried them back towards cover and continued past Mitch and Leah, eager to put distance and buildings between them and whatever threat lay up ahead.

After a while, he stopped and laid the wounded man on the ground against a low wall. All three were out of breath, and Dan began to assess the injury.

A bullet had passed through his left side, just above the hip and miraculously missing the vital organs only inches away. Dan reached inside the injured man's clothing to check for an exit wound on his back, prompting a cry of anguish.

Leah burst into his view and Dan glanced up to see Mitch adopting a new position to face the direction they had come from. The girl snatched a dressing from a pouch on her vest, having seen the blood-blackening clothing in the moonlight.

"Through and through," muttered Dan. "Nothing internal by the feel of it," he said to her in a low voice. He left the girl to patch the ragged wound as best as she could in the dark and pulled Simon away. The man was breathing heavily, barely able to catch his breath.

"What happened?" hissed Dan.

"Bastards came for us when it got dark," he said through ragged breathing. "It was Riley who led them to us," he finished.

"Why?" Dan asked, suspecting that he could guess the answer, having seen the petulant jealousy evident on the man when he had met him earlier.

"We argued over what to do," Simon replied. He spoke too loudly and received a warning to keep his voice down. "So the bastard tried to organise a coup," Simon said, quieter this time.

Dan let him catch his breath, waiting for more of the story to unfold.

"Nobody would follow him in the end, so he left," he said. He bent double and put his face in his hands. "I had no idea he was going to go straight to them and say where we were," he finished, dumbstruck at the savage turn of events.

Dan's anger flashed inside him, reminding him that he couldn't help but interject in the injustices of the lives of others. It was one of his biggest character flaws that he couldn't simply mind his own business sometimes.

"How many?" he asked in a low voice filled with loathing.

Simon stopped panting and fixed Dan with a look of almost desperate terror. "Everyone," he said lamely.

Not counting Riley, Simon and his injured friend, the betrayal had cost the lives of seven men. The senseless loss of life made Dan livid with rage. He wanted to walk in there right now and end every last one of them.

But for what? For defending their resources against other armed men? For sneaking into another camp and killing people who threatened them?

For doing what Dan had himself done to others?

He shook himself out of his pointless murderous mood, forcing his concentration back to the immediate.

"We need to get him back to our group," Dan said. "He needs more medical help than we can give here or he won't make it."

"We do," growled Leah in frustration as she packed dressings into the twin bullet holes. "I can't stop the bleeding with what I have. We need Kate."

Dan reckoned they'd need Sera more, with her knowledge of surgery being more in-depth than Kate's, but didn't think the difference was worth pointing out there and then. The man was breathing in shallow, rapid gasps and had gone very quiet. Only infrequent and weak yelps escaped his lips now as the teenager tried to keep pressure on his wounds. He was going into shock and was not going to make it out here.

He turned and gave the familiar short, low whistle to signal Mitch. The soldier leapt up and ran to him.

"Through and through to the abdomen. Going into shock. We need to carry him back."

Mitch absorbed the information instantly, passing Dan his carbine as he hauled the man up and threw him on his shoulder into a fireman's lift. Leah went ahead, scanning for danger as Dan walked backwards to maintain a rearguard. Their progress back to the bay was far slower than their first leg, but luckily there seemed to be no pursuit.

After an eternity struggling slowly through the dark, they returned to the steps leading from the water to their borrowed house. Another whistle indicated to them that their house guards had seen them appear. More help arrived, and the now unconscious man was carried up the steps to be laid on the large, expensive dining table.

Food tins and bottles were scattered as space was cleared, and Kate shouted for everyone to get out of her way.

Instinctively, Sera ran to her side as Leah gave the report.

"Entry and exit wound, left side. I can't stop the bleeding."

Kate nodded as she produced a heavy set of medical shears and cut away the clothing before pulling back the dressings Leah had packed onto the victim. Blood welled up instantly and spilled over the side of the table to cascade to the expensive white-tiled floor, the beauty of the awful juxtaposition both captivating and horrific.

Kate pressed the dressing back down firmly and barked orders at stunned people foolish enough to be in her line of sight as she worked.

"Cushions; elevate his feet," she snapped at a very pale Henry.

To his credit, he immediately switched on and did as he was told.

Sera took up the mantle and ordered two others to find towels. She laid a brief hand on Kate's shoulder and said that she would fetch their equipment. Ash whined and backpedalled to the side of the room as he sensed the urgency and fear in his humans.

Dan withdrew, leaving those with the knowledge to do what they did best. If anyone could save this man's life, it was the fearless paramedic and her frosty vet partner.

Neil and Adam had stayed outside to defend the building, and he nodded to Leah and Mitch to join them. Both went without a word.

He met Simon's eye and gestured for him to follow to the balcony where he had been standing when he had first heard the shots.

NOT EVERY BATTLE IS YOURS TO FIGHT

Dan stood and lit a cigarette, ignoring the blood already crusting on his shaking hands. It wasn't fear, he knew that – it was the body purging the excess adrenaline from his system. He was all too familiar with the physiological reaction to a life-threatening situation, unlike after his debut battle where he had vomited uncontrollably after the first time he had ever pulled a trigger in anger.

His dog came to his side and nuzzled him for reassurance. Simon stood in front of him with a stony, lifeless expression. "They swarmed in and just started shooting," he said quietly, deflated and empty. "We didn't stand a chance. We just ran and tried to hide. Some of us managed to shoot back for a while, but there were too many of them."

Of course they didn't stand a chance, thought Dan. They probably didn't even place sentries. They probably camped too close to an enemy. They were farmers, not warriors.

"Me and Al were shooting back, trying to get some others out, but when he got shot, I just picked him up and ran." He hung his head, the realisation that his actions felt like cowardice suddenly stinging him.

"If you hadn't, then you'd all be dead," Dan responded calmly, trying to avoid an emotional meltdown in the big man.

"All of this over some bloody fuel," Simon cursed angrily, "like people didn't have enough to fight over before!"

The irony of the situation was not lost on Dan; it seemed even the last remnants of the human race were destined to go to war over fossil fuels.

"And now they're dead. For nothing. We were going to leave in the morning, so God only knows what the bastard Riley told them our plans were."

The full force of the loss hit him, and he cried shamelessly. He sunk to the floor and sat there. Dan left him for a while to get it out of his system, ever awkward around others' emotions.

On looking back inside the house, Dan could see that the man on the table was still subject to a desperate flurry of attention to try and save his life. His eyes met Marie's as she wordlessly invited an explanation with raised eyebrows. He flicked his cigarette behind him for it to fly into the dark abyss of the shimmering harbour like a solitary firework in the distance.

He walked back inside and saw her look of annoyance at the red stains covering his hands. She snatched up a pack of baby wipes and began to scrub at the dried blood obsessively as he talked, as though being busy and clean could make this whole mess go away. He told her everything he knew in a succinct report, avoiding investing his words with the impotent anger he felt.

"Well, we need to get away from here as soon as possible," she said.

For once, Dan agreed. Never one to run away from a fight, he had no intention of trying to take on an overwhelming force with only a few soldiers experienced in the exchange of bullets. His attention was violently torn away from their conversation as he heard a shout of "Fuck!" from the dining area.

He turned to see Kate giving chest compressions to the man, knowing the outcome already, as the man's exposed skin showed almost clear from the blood loss.

She shouted for the defibrillator to be brought, and Dan stepped in to take over the CPR while she set it up.

Over the next minute, she tried four shocks from the automated machine as everyone stood clear in resigned silence as they followed the instructions from the electronic voice.

She gave up, finally admitting that he couldn't be saved. People melted away, some in tears and others in quiet shock. Without being asked, Henry brought a fresh bed sheet from an airing cupboard and laid it over the man with a maturity and reverence that Dan didn't realise he possessed. Henry seemed a little embarrassed by his actions and went red. Dan recognised the decent thing that he had done and laid a hand on his shoulder as he passed, returning to Marie.

She tut-tutted again and began to work with the wipes to remove the fresh blood on the recently cleaned skin. It was no good; the dark liquid had worked its way into the creases of his rough hands and stubbornly refused to budge. She stopped wasting her efforts.

"We need to leave," she said again as she poked a stern finger into his ballistic vest, before turning away to check on the others.

A look around the room saw people hugging each other. For many, this would be the first time they had seen such a sight. For others, the repetition would be no easier to stomach.

He stood outside the front door and gave the whistle to recall his sentries. He left Neil to guard the door and asked Leah to fetch her big rifle with its light-enhancing scope to take the balcony overlooking the area. Both nodded without a word and went to fetch what they needed for the first stint of a night shift.

Kate and Sera were wrapping the man in the sheet and cleaning up the detritus of torn dressing packs. Ana had started to clean up the blood on the floor. Everywhere he looked, he saw his gang rapidly getting over the experience and moving on with their lives. Despite the awful gravity of the evening's events, he felt a small surge of pride for how resilient they were, and he hoped that he hadn't let them down by asking them to follow him.

Henry, having already impressed Dan, made the world a far better place by his next move. He lit the camping cooker in the kitchen and set some water to boil.

Leah returned, having added an extra layer of clothing, and moved the balcony tables together to form a firing platform she could lie down on, adding a roll mat to the top and settling in to nestle the huge rifle against her cheek. To be such a professional at that age was a marvel for Dan to watch. He gave her shoulder a squeeze as she settled in to get comfortable.

He brought Simon inside and sat him on the plush sofa as Marie appeared to take over. He was cleaned up, fresh clothes were found to replace the bloodstained ones he wore, and a hot drink was placed gently in his hands. Henry made the rounds, dishing out cups of black coffee to others. He took a cup to Leah, who grunted a sullen thanks to the boy who stared at her too much for her liking.

Dan found himself looking into the eager eyes of the boy who was holding a cup out to him.

"Black. Strong. No sugar," he said, almost desperate for praise.

"Good lad," said Dan, meaning more than just making him a drink.

"No problem," he said as he walked away, trying to hide his evident pride, "boss," he added sheepishly.

TIME TO GO

The night went by slowly. After four hours of fitful rest, Dan took over from Leah, and Mitch relieved Neil. Adam was kept out of the night shift, as he was the only one of their fighters to be inexperienced. Plus, he would do the heavy lifting during the day to make up for it.

Simon was still walking around like a ghost at daybreak, having slept in the seat he occupied after coming inside. Dan spoke with him for a while, finding out what he wanted to do.

Another strong coffee was placed in Dan's hand as the group assembled to tuck into the box of breakfast bars and tins of fruit placed on the table, which now smelled strongly of bleach after Ana had eradicated all traces of the tragic scene there only hours ago. Everyone looked tired, with the exception of Neil and Mitch, who seemed not to require sleep like normal humans.

"Right," said Dan loudly, silencing the chatter and gaining everyone's attention. "Last night was not pleasant," he said, understating something which a couple of years ago would have left most people traumatised for life. "But there's no way we can stay around here, nor can we consider trying to get at the diesel in the boatyard. There are too many of them and they have too many guns. We're avoiding any fighting at all costs."

That seemed to relax everyone. Dan outlined that they still needed diesel, but that the game had changed. They had to leave the harbour as soon as they could, and it was suggested that they move further down the coast away from danger.

"We load everything onto the boat and Mitch will take most people out onto the water to shadow us west. The others will come with me and bring the vehicles. We use the hand pumps to collect every bit of fuel we can; we fill the cars, the reserve tank on the Land Rover and the jerrycans. We fill the boat with as much as we can and then we fill the Land Rover up again and Simon will take it home with Al's body to be buried with his family."

He let that sink in before continuing. "Pack up; everyone on the boat except the following." He listed names, deciding to include Henry to put his eagerness to please to good use.

The air of happy excitement had totally evaporated after the elation of their arrival in the bay. Without ceremony, the supplies were loaded on board and those chosen not to engage in the fuelling tasks shuffled down the jetty to climb up to the deck of *Hope*.

Dan nodded to Mitch, who slowly piloted them out into the waters of the wide bay. Dan turned to his assembled team of ten and issued assignments.

For the next two hours, they mostly walked from vehicle to vehicle siphoning off every bit of diesel they could find. Jerrycans were filled and passed up to the roof of the Defender, where the precious liquid was carefully decanted into the large reserve tank originally fitted for Steve to take Emma to Scotland.

As the sun neared its peak, Dan called a halt for them to rest. He reckoned they had got close to a thousand litres by now by topping up the spare cans and tanks. Adam went ahead with Leah, as both seemed eternally restless to scout for more. They returned after twenty minutes wearing broad smiles; they had located another source of jerrycans and a fuel station.

Within an hour, Neil had rigged a pump to extra hoses and they took turns in emptying the reservoir. With all of their containers full, they loaded up and continued on to the next point where they reached the water easily. It took all afternoon to reverse the journey of the fuel into the cans and carry it to be poured into the tank on the boat.

After that, Dan took one of the motorbikes strapped to the back where the jet ski would have sat at the stern of the boat and went with Simon to return to their diesel source. They pumped more in to fill the tanks in silence.

Simon took the fuel and his new vehicle containing the body of his friend, bid a quiet goodbye, and drove north without another word.

By the time Dan returned to the boat, the sun was already sinking. Adam and Leah had cleared a nearby building, although one of far lower status than their home of yesterday, and the group settled down as the light faded for a night of waiting for the sun to rise.

THE CALMING

The period of disorder had faded after a couple of days. Apologies were made between quarrelling parties and the mood, although sombre, had at least returned to civility.

Steve still remained motionless in medical. He was watched around the clock, and the clear bag hanging from the side of his bed continued to fill with bloody urine as the fluids entering his system through the needle in his arm cycled through his battered body. Lizzie and Alice did the best they could, but there was no way of telling if he would ever wake up.

As far as they knew, he was in a coma – a fact that they tried to keep from the others, bar the council. Lexi shared the story of the day Dan and Leah found them, of how he had given peace to an injured man who would never wake up. She tried hard to remember the man's name, and even harder to put the similarities out of her head.

Combined with the loss of some of their most valued people and the catastrophic wreckage of Steve's return, people were quite simply depressed. The world still turned. People got up and went to work. Food was reared, grown, prepared and eaten. Just not with the same sense of purpose as it once had. The belief that they were the last generation of people to exist on the planet seemed to have finally sunk in, and that realisation brought with it an air of futility.

They experienced their first suicide the following morning.

One of the group originally rescued from Bronson's prison was found when he was late reporting for work on the gardens. He had hanged himself in his room, leaving a note which spoke simply of the pointlessness of life. Another subdued burial ceremony took place, only this time half of the remaining group attended. Precious few words were spoken as the handfuls of dirt were dropped onto the shrouded body.

Lexi and Paul had taken over Dan and Marie's room, not wanting to let sentiment affect valuable real estate. They lay there that night, neither able to sleep until both realised that the other was still wide awake.

"Can't sleep?" she asked softly.

"No," he replied in a whisper. "Can I ask you a question?" he said after a pause.

"Yes," she said, and before he could ask it, she answered, "We should have gone with them."

SET SAIL

Morning brought with it a hive of activity. The ability of people to compartmentalise and move on from bad experiences never ceased to amaze Dan, even though he had been through more than enough himself and still survived. And that was before the world had ended.

Water was boiled, caffeine was infused into bodies and again Henry made sure to deliver hot coffee to Dan and Leah. The idolisation was becoming embarrassing, but nowhere near enough to turn down coffee.

Mitch called for everyone's attention from the higher deck and faced the assembled group. With satirical ceremony, he invited everyone to board *Hope*, and with a lavish gesture, he produced a white captain's hat and put it on with comedy extravagance. It got the expected laughs, and Dan noticed an annoyed look on Neil's face. As the resident intentional clown, he didn't take kindly to being up-staged.

Everyone and everything was aboard, supplies and bags were all squared away, and people found places to sit. Most crowded onto the main deck to watch their own departure.

In keeping with the high mood, the now co-captains of Mitch and Neil stood up on the upper steering deck and the boat's horn sounded as they gathered speed out into the huge harbour.

It became obvious to Dan just how foolish this was.

None of them had the first idea about sailing, and if the boat hadn't had controls like a very large automatic car, then he doubted they would have even been able to drive it.

Or sail it, or whatever it was called.

The thought dawned on him that during their planning phase, not one person had suggested driving through the Channel Tunnel. He cast that aside as an irrelevance now.

The excitement of their departure was dampened by the fact that it took them nearly twenty minutes to navigate their way around the island which sat silent in the mouth of the entrance to the harbour. Dan was struck again by the beauty of the world when it was viewed unspoiled by humans, the brooding sentry obstructing their path to stand guard over the exit to their small piece of home soil.

Turning right out of the mouth of the watery haven, the engine was opened up to take advantage of the uninhibited stretch of calm water. As they ploughed on into heavier waves, Dan saw some looking behind at the slowly diminishing English coastline. Excitement and fear, adventure and trepidation. All these emotions competed for attention in his consciousness, but the decision was made. Their path was, for now, set, and they were under way, heading south with the rising sun bathing them with warmth on their left sides.

Jack came up from below deck with a fishing rod and weighted lure, where he proceeded to settle himself on the seat of a motorbike tied down tight and cast off into their wake. Dan wondered if he had any expectation of catching anything or merely wanted to offer some small entertainment.

After about twenty minutes, the excitement of their departure from the mainland had worn off entirely and people began to find comfortable places to spend the day.

Dan climbed the metal ladder to find Mitch and Neil arguing good-naturedly about their course. The plan was simple: head for France and turn left.

At least, he hoped it would be that simple.

THE BLIND LEADING THE ENTHUSI-ASTIC

Heading south into the relatively calm English Channel, the group talked excitedly for the first hour until nobody could clearly make out the land masses either in front of them or behind. The co-captains had agreed on a heading which led them slightly east of south and should take them to the closest part of France from where they had set off.

If it went according to plan, they should be seeing Cherbourg ahead of them inside of three or four hours. That declaration was made without either Mitch's or Neil's characteristic confidence, but Dan had looked at the maps too. It should work.

He spent much of the early part of the journey helping Leah with their most difficult passenger. In stark contrast to Jack, who had fallen asleep within thirty minutes of departure and still hadn't moved, one of their most valuable members was whimpering as he threw up violently with every unexpected motion.

It was alien to Ash; he'd never had a problem with carsickness before, but other than walking, it was the only method of travel he had ever experienced. Worse than the sickness were the noises he made; genuine fear was expressed, as he couldn't understand why every time he tried to stand, his legs didn't feel like his own and betrayed him. He flopped around the foredeck, retching onto the white surfaces of the boat like a newborn deer after drinking shots.

He only got worse as their boat hit the wide open shipping lanes where the water was deepest, until he finally passed out from the exhaustion.

"I'll keep an eye on him," said Leah as she shuffled the big dog into a better position and wiped some foul-smelling bile from her hands on the leg of her black combats.

"Thanks," Dan replied, "just try to get him to drink something when he wakes up."

The efficient teenager nodded to him as he left. He placed a hand on her shoulder to notionally help himself up, but really to express the emotion he felt for her while lacking the words.

A shout from above made him turn to see Neil pointing ahead of them as the haze to the south began to form features and morph into a distant landscape.

They had reached France.

They were probably some of the few people since it happened to have done this, to have escaped their own isolated island and break out to another country.

Dan was under no illusion that they were anywhere close to their destination yet; if they landed there, then they faced a journey of hundreds of miles across country to where they were aiming for in Germany. The urge to get back on dry land was strong, but he had to avoid that pull and make good ground – or water – while they could.

Climbing the ladder to the upper deck, he relieved Neil, who was feeling the strain of being at the controls. Mitch, in contrast, never seemed to tire. Dan supposed it was the way he had lived his life as an infantryman; often, Mitch would grab five or ten minutes' sleep here and there and wake refreshed, like he had rapid-charging lithium ion batteries when everyone else ran on solar power.

The heavy sea walls of the ferry port came into view shortly afterwards, prompting Dan to swing the boat further east and cut out a large stretch of the curved coastline. A huge cross-Channel ferry lay dead in the port, massive and hulking against the shoreline and destined to rot there until she finally sank to the shallow bottom.

They cruised steadily, enjoying calmer seas for a time as they kept the sandy beaches and buildings of the French coast at a distance. Mitch opined that keeping out to this distance from the shore would save the need to avoid any outcrops of rocks, eager to display some knowledge of the subject to cover the many things he didn't know. One of those was how to use the radar detection equipment designed for such dangers. Their mechanic, Phil, could have been some help, only he was as bad as Ash and had spent most of the day hanging his head over the guard rail at the stern. He had the knack of making any device work easily – when he wasn't being sick.

Jack opened his eyes enough to thank him for attracting some fish for him to catch, before he nodded off again.

Leah joined them on the deck, having anticipated Dan's concerns by telling him that Marie was watching Ash after he had raised his eyebrows on seeing her; she always knew when he was going to ask a stupid question.

She unfolded a map and tried to hold it flat against the pull of the wind. She bent over it with Dan and tried to estimate where they were. It wasn't too difficult, as they could see the outstretched landmark of Cherbourg behind them. Best guesses were that they had maybe another three hours cruising the French coastline.

"Want a go, kid?" Mitch asked her with a broad smile, eager for a break himself.

There was a time not too long ago when she would have said no, would have shied away from such a responsibility. More recently, there was a time when she would have looked to Dan for permission. No longer, it seemed.

"Hell yes!" she said, stepping up and receiving instructions on power and direction. All she had to do was hold it steady and not hit anything, and seeing as they were in calm, empty waters, she doubted that was a problem.

Dan stayed and watched her, making a show of consulting the map but really just enjoying seeing his protégé relish the freedom of being at the controls. After a while, he gave up on his ruse and stepped back to smoke and openly gaze at her as she made deft minor corrections to their course. If he allowed himself only to think of this moment, and not the risks or the reasons for their journey, then he had to admit that he was actually enjoying himself.

Until a yelp and whine from his seasick dog answered by retching and coughing from Phil at the back of the boat brought him back to reality with nauseating efficiency.

THE SEA LIVES IN EVERY ONE OF US

"That's what I heard, anyway!" shouted Neil almost absentmindedly as he fought to stay upright at the controls. Dan would wager that right now, every one of their group felt no affinity for the sea whatsoever.

He could tell that Neil's attempt at small talk was masking a healthy dose of fear because he delivered the half-remembered quote without any trace of an accent or impression. *He must be feeling the stress*, Dan thought.

For the last three parts of an hour, they had been buffeted, bombarded and battered in a sudden squall which showed little sign of abating. Just as Mitch was lecturing Leah on the history of the wide beaches off to her right – Utah, Omaha, Gold – the weather closed in with such rapid savagery that their dreams of a calm summer crossing were metaphorically dashed upon the rocks. It had got much worse in a very short period of time.

Most passengers were inside below decks, and all but a few were unwell. Very quickly, the multimillion-pound yacht started to smell like a stairwell in an undesirable block of flats. Only Dan and Leah remained above decks with Neil and Mitch, fighting to keep the controls steady.

The stupidity of trying to cross the Channel hit Dan again, and he chose safety over progress without hesitation. It was about as sensible as driving a van on the motorway after having two lessons in a go-kart.

"Get us into port somewhere!" he shouted over the sudden howling wind to his rain-soaked men.

Mitch turned the boat with a gut-churning lurch as he timed it wrong and a wave hit their left side to move them unnaturally.

Stupid and *dangerous*, thought Dan. Not one of them had enough knowledge or experience of seamanship to risk all their lives on this reckless course. They had to get to safety, and soon. The weather wasn't that bad in the grand scheme of things, but trying to control such a large vessel with no experience was turning the situation from bad to worse.

Trying to get the boat safely moored would pose yet more danger, but Dan could bear the risk of inactivity no longer. Wishing he had called a stop that afternoon after they passed what he guessed was the next main ferry port at Ouistreham, he cursed his mistakes again. Sacrificing safety for speed would not work.

Truth was, he had desperately underestimated how long it would take to mirror the French coastline, and was already almost half a day behind where he thought they would be. Again, he toyed with the choices: get on dry land and find uncertain transport or continue by sea and risk drowning them all over their nautical inadequacies.

Land. He needed land. He was too stressed, too fearful of the sea to work out the figures.

Another day by water and one hundred and fifty miles was their current plan. The alternative plan that he had chosen, not that he could have calculated this without a map and plenty of quiet time, was an overland journey of around five hundred miles to their next destination.

Five hundred miles with no guarantee of finding working vehicles. Five hundred miles of uncertain food supplies. Five hundred miles of scavenging for fuel.

Regardless of all the uncertainty, the terror of the water bore down on him just as he worried a rogue wave would at any time. He turned to Leah.

"Go below, carefully! Tell everyone we're going to find somewhere safe to stop!" he shouted to Leah over the unseasonably high winds.

She nodded and nimbly shimmied down the tubular ladder. Her lightweight and agile frame seemed to make her less susceptible to the debilitating forces of physics, it seemed.

Dan stayed with Neil and Mitch as they now headed due south, with waves catching them up from behind every twenty seconds and pushing them forward in sickening surges. They couldn't tell because of the gathering dark and the stinging rain, but they were almost four miles out to sea and not a single person aboard wholly believed that they would make it to safety.

SECOND FIRST RANGER

Lexi didn't feel much like the military faction leader of the group.

She felt like a fraud, in fact.

Her lessons to the new recruits on weapon drills and techniques were all half-remembered lessons passed on by Dan. She had sufficient skills herself, but she lacked the experience and ability to recognise talent in others and bring it out. She simply did not feel up to the task.

This apathy for her current role became evident in her manner towards the others who were halfheartedly receiving her instructions and in turn led to a pointless exercise where nobody learned a damn thing.

Seeing that the group under her instruction had switched off, and failing to recognise that she was at fault, she sent them away testily after ensuring that they had all made safe their weapons. Angrily, she cleared all of the pistols left on the makeshift bench of a downed tree, gathered up the rounds and weapons and walked back to the house. She dumped the armful of mixed weaponry carelessly in front of Rich, who was sitting at the table in Ops, and walked out without saying a word.

She went to her room and paced alone. Realising that this was doing nothing for her mood, she paced back through the house and out of the back doors to cross the garden towards the gym. Cutting through the treeline, she burst through the doors looking for Paul. One look at her face told him that she was very unhappy, although he mistook that look for anger when it would more easily have become tears. She paced again as she vented to him, detailing her fears and the obstacles facing them. How could she possibly fill Dan's shoes? Why did Steve have to get hurt? Why couldn't she just do her job? Why did she have to be in charge?

All of these thoughts and more poured from her like lava until she finally cracked and the tears burst from her like a dam breaking. She cried in Paul's arms, who unlike Dan knew how to listen and hug a woman instead of trying to fix every problem. They stayed like that for some time until she stood up, put her brave face back on, and told him they were going out.

Equally as unwilling to communicate, Rich sighed and picked up the first of the weapons which lay scattered on his neat work space. He began the long process of stripping and cleaning each component; while not strictly necessary, it took up the next hour of his life with useful distraction.

He knew things were falling apart. He could see it from the moment Dan announced that he was leaving. The helicopter crash was what had affected him most, however.

The brutality of it. The noise. The memories it brought back to him.

He hadn't slept more than a few hours in the last five days; terrible images and sounds came to him when he did, and it was best not to think about it too much.

A slow and surreptitious check of his surroundings reassured him that he was the only one in earshot, allowing him the peace and privacy to take a long and meaningful gulp from the bottle hidden in the desk drawer.

With a shaking hand, he returned the cork, wiped his mouth, and remembered just how good it felt to have the fiery drink burning its way down his gullet and into his stomach, where the fierce liquid radiated heat and numbness outwards to even the missing fingers of his right hand.

As he stood there bathing in the warm glow, Lexi walked back in, snatched up her weapons and went to leave. She paused, sniffed the air a couple of times, and walked out.

"Me and Paul are going out," she said curtly. "Back by nightfall."

Lexi relaxed slightly as she strode outside, racking a round into the chamber of her rifle. She climbed behind the wheel of Dan's Discovery – her Discovery now – and waited as Paul climbed in beside her, and then she drove away hard up the long lane leading away from the house that used to be a happy place.

IMPERFECT LANDING

It had taken another thirty minutes to reach the coastline, by which time some of the passengers below deck were now openly certain of a watery death. Marie had done her best to calm the most nervous, but between her early stages of pregnancy and so many people being sick, she too soon succumbed to the situation.

Henry, remarkably, was proving to be a worthy addition to the group, despite initially being a stowaway and almost being sent back. He went among the worried and the ill with water and words of reassurance. It seemed that the only useful members were now the two youngest, as he and Leah made sure everyone was still with them. Even the ever stoic and indestructible Jack was looking deathly pale and muttering intensely with his eyes closed, running rosary beads between forefinger and thumb.

Henry tried to give a companionable nod and place a nonchalant hand on the shoulder of Leah, resulting in an equally casual wrist lock and removal of the unwanted appendage. Henry wordlessly got the point and retreated to rub his sore joints.

Above deck, even Dan had been bested by the weather and had vomited down the side of the boat. Luckily, the driving rain had washed it away quickly. Through a break in the storm clouds, Mitch shouted incoherently and pointed ahead and to their left – a break in the beach where a wide inlet flowed inland and signified safety from the elements. Slowly, the nose of the boat shifted to point directly at their new haven. A further ten minutes saw them throttling back so as not to approach too fast. Floating debris blocked their path – small fishing boats had been ruined by neglect and the elements, but parts of them were still anchored to the flat bottom of the bay. Little could be done to avoid hitting them, as the shallow seabed was littered with similar wreckage.

Terrible noises reverberated around the vessel as they bumped and screeched their way into calmer waters, each noise prompting shouts of panic and alarm as well as screams and tears of fear.

Leah was treated to one of her personal moments of slow-time reverie; glancing between the door of the cabin and Henry, she was certain that she would do the same as the woman in the film she saw about a shipwreck. There was no way she was sharing her bit of floating door with a boy.

Her feelings and senses surrounding mortality were simpler than most people's, it seemed.

The sounds of contact with something other than the angry sea and their reduction in speed made Leah return topside. She found that they had made land and were creeping into a mess of a wide river with bits of boats everywhere. The water was infinitely calmer inside the bay, and a glance behind her showed furious waves crashing against the coastline.

Dan had recovered sufficiently to offer her a mirthless welcome to France as she climbed to the upper deck. They had entered the river mouth and turned right with the flow. Directly in front of them was a marina that seemed to be a graveyard for so many small boats. Being in the protected waters had preserved them slightly, but none had survived undamaged without human attention. Dan pointed them to keep right and follow the river as it looped a lazy arc to the left and passed under a road bridge. They covered another mile or so at slow speeds to avoid the now less common obstacles before they saw small piers on their right.

Dan guessed they were probably the more private moorings of the expensive houses, not massively dissimilar to their luxurious temporary home in Poole Harbour. As Mitch guided *Hope* in towards the sturdy jetty, Dan and Leah prepared to jump ashore and tie the boat steady. It took some difficulty and the engine had to be back-geared to prevent it overshooting the mooring, but eventually they were safe.

This far inland, the surface of the water merely moved instead of roiling violently as it did outside of the bay. Slowly, their passengers began to emerge from below decks and seek the psychological sanctuary of solid ground. Henry emerged rubbing his hand at a mark already showing red. He admitted to Dan that he tried to help by carrying Ash outside, and although weakened by his first journey by sea, the dog had retained sufficient wherewithal to land a successful bite on him.

Dan cuffed the young lad around the ear for being foolish and told him to wash the bite thoroughly; he hadn't broken the skin, but Dan had seen how quickly dog bites became infections.

He carried the grey dog outside himself, resting him gently down on the wet ground and watching him regain his unsteady footing. Leaving the main members of the group to recover under the watchful eyes of Adam, Neil and Mitch, he nodded his head to Leah to indicate that they should secure the wider area.

Carbines up, knees bent and moving at an efficient crouch, the two covered distance between buildings while maintaining a covering arc on the other. Hours they had spent drilling this, both for real and in practice. The only thing missing was the dog at his heel, although the dog could barely stand upright for now, so they would have to do without him.

Windows were checked, signs of life were looked for and nothing was found. The immediate area was dominated by boat sheds and store rooms for fishing and sailing equipment, but after that came a wide road which opened out onto an intricate line of zigzagged buildings, three and four storeys high. They appeared to be apartment blocks, with jutted windows and irregular angles protruding. In itself, the building was nothing special, but the contrasting angles and colours mesmerised Dan briefly until he switched on again and bent to the sight of his carbine.

He had fitted a new sight before they left, the one where the zoom lens was optional and could be clicked aside, revealing a red dot sight for close quarters work. Naturally, Leah had followed suit almost immediately and fitted the same hardware to her own camouflage-dappled gun.

Ten minutes of moving and checking streets showed no signs that anyone still inhabited this town, and resisting the temptation to explore the overgrown leafy residential roads led them back to the boatyard.

Adam had let them into a large single-story building which appeared to have been some kind of office or centre for the marina. People were making themselves more comfortable and preparing for a night on solid ground. Water was being boiled, clothes were being changed, and slowly the smell of vomit was becoming less prevalent as other smells competed for attention.

The smell of coffee cut through the mess of aromas to trigger something in Dan to remind him how acutely tired he felt. True to form, Henry appeared with two cups and made straight for them. Dan thanked him and accepted one. Leah grunted something vaguely approaching thanks and took the other before walking off. The red welt on the boy's arm looked painful, but he did not complain.

Ash had recovered greatly and made a nervous and slightly wobbly run at him with his head down and his tail wagging. Dan dropped to one knee and slung his weapon behind his back as he fussed his huge dog like a baby, much to the amusement of those watching.

The fearless warrior. The terrifying dog. Both killers, but both obviously big softies who cared a great deal for the other. It was as though one wasn't truly complete without the other.

He sipped his drink and watched his little group again; he really had the cream of the crop with him, he marvelled. Not one person ever waited for instruction; nobody had to be told to get something or had to be asked for help. These people had chosen to follow him for whatever their personal reasons were, all working well together.

Another fragrant note hit his nostrils, as unwelcome as it was to many who still suffered with acidic stomachs: food.

He wandered towards the smell and found Neil showing Pip his speciality.

"Whole tin of potatoes, whole tin of steak, and a whole tin of carrots," he said flamboyantly in a lisping London accent, no doubt mimicking some celebrity chef who Dan probably wouldn't have heard of. "Bring it to the boil, whisk it up nice and fast, and then crack in your eggs," he finished as he cracked three eggs onto the spinning pot of brown liquid showing occasional flashes of orange.

"Mountaineering Spew," announced Dan, simultaneously embarrassing and annoying Neil by ruining his punch line. "We made that on our very first night together," he finished with a rueful smile.

How the world had changed so many times since these two had first bumped into each other.

THE CHOICES WE MAKE...

As dark settled, so too did the group. The mood had picked up in the few hours since they had sought refuge on dry land, after the nausea and the fear had abated.

Ash was now fully alert and able to maintain his balance. His day of vomiting had made his insatiable hunger for other people's food worse than ever, so much so that he had eaten an entire bowl of dog food and instantly gone to seek more sustenance from the helpless humans who looked at him with wide eyes as he stood staring at them. Slowly, carefully, most of them relented and gave him some of their food. Satisfied, he moved on to the next victim and the tension he left behind evaporated. Dan realised that he was terrorising the group with his personal version of minesweeping, and ruined his entertainment by calling him to heel, effectively ending his tyrannical search for snacks.

He upset Ash further still as he took him outside for his turn to keep watch. Dan sat huddled inside a small shelter throughout the evening, interrupted only by the occasional cup of coffee being brought to him and with it small snippets of conversation.

Pip was scared that they wouldn't make it after the weather closed in, and Dan tried not to show that he had felt exactly the same. Others were worried about going back to sea too. He listened, but made no assurances.

Neil came to relieve him, with Mitch due to take over in the early hours; the two men usually worked it like that, as they both bizarrely functioned well on little sleep. Dan knew that would only work for a short amount of time before tiredness became physical exhaustion. He spoke with Neil and canvassed his thoughts on their options: chance it by road from here or try to get further east along the coastline to be closer to their intended target.

Neil was characteristically nonchalant about such matters; he was just happy to be along for the ride. This time, however, as much as he couldn't face the thought of going back out to sea, he knew what the right course of action was.

Dan gave up his shelter to the older man and walked stiffly back towards their temporary home as he stretched his muscles. He took a lap of the low building to smoke, ease his cramped muscles and exercise his dog a little before joining the others inside.

He was handed a hot drink as he walked in, thanked the person who offered it and scanned the room for Marie. He caught sight of her making the rounds and raising the morale of their band. He was mesmerised by the way she moved among their small group, placing a hand on a shoulder here, laughing at a comment there. He marvelled at the way she brought out the very best in everyone and shone a little light into whatever dark there was. He wasn't so ignorant to realise that those who had followed weren't there just for him; some had come because of her, and he knew why. She was still as captivating to him as the first time he'd laid eyes on her.

As he reminisced about that first meeting, her eyes found his. A warm smile showed, and he moved towards her. An embrace, the reassurance of physical contact, welcomed him back into the warm. They spoke briefly before Dan turned to the assembled party.

"Meeting time, people," he said loudly, "everyone in."

Mutters and mumbles emanated from the assembly. Small noises of excitement rose from them as everyone shuffled closer together to hear what he had to say before an eventual hush descended.

"I'm sure we're all happy to be back on dry land after today," he began, getting the nervous laughter he expected. "Truth is, nobody was expecting bad weather this late in summer, and it wasn't even that bad as far as things go, but it's just that none of us are really the sailing type!"

That was an understatement. He pressed on, eager to hear the collective views instead of forcing his will on everyone. "We now face a choice," he said, leaving the words to hang heavy. "We can go back out to sea tomorrow and stick to our original plan, or we can try to go across country from here. Now, I don't expect anyone to decide without knowing the facts; you know me well enough by now. Leah?"

The girl pushed herself away from the wall where she lounged like a resting predator and came to stand beside him. A glance upwards showed that she didn't like the height difference, so she kicked over a small wooden box and stood on top to better be seen.

"As far as I can work out from the map, we're looking at over five hundred miles across country." Dan had discussed this with her earlier and seen her hard at work with a map and a small length of string which she used to calculate the distance by snaking it along the major road markings and into Germany.

"Or another day – maybe two – back at sea and only about a quarter of that distance by road," finished Dan. "Despite not liking today's experience, I think it's going to be quicker to go by sea, but probably safer to go slowly by land."

Marie took over, not needing the height advantage that Leah did.

"The journey by land will mean that we will spend a few days at least scavenging for food and fuel as we go. We can't be sure of finding good enough vehicles either."

The group sat silently. While Dan was eager to give them their own choice to decide their way, most would happily submit to whatever he suggested.

He didn't want that added burden. He wanted someone else to decide something for once so the responsibility wasn't his every time.

Jack held up a hand. "Back out to sea," he said in his gruff Belfast accent. "It's still summer and we shouldn't see too much more of the bad weather. Today was just unlucky, is all."

Murmurs of agreement, as well as some tight-lipped silence.

"Let's just get it over with, shall we?" said Mitch. "One more day and then it's done."

Naturally, Adam agreed with him. As did a few more of the group.

Eager to have the decision made, Dan asked for a show of hands. "Back to the boat?" he asked.

Ten hands rose. Counting Neil's proxy vote for sea travel made the significant majority.

"By land?" Only a few raised their objections, most of whom were the ones who had suffered crippling bouts of seasickness. Dan could understand that.

"By sea, then," he said. "Sorry to those who didn't want it that way but I promise it'll be over soon. Get some rest, everybody. Early start ahead."

With that, Leah jumped lithely down from her pedestal and joined him and Marie as they settled down to try and sleep.

BEWARE THE FURY OF A PATIENT MAN

He had never done anything like this in his life, nor had he even contemplated it.

This wasn't him at all, only it was him now. The injustice of it, the treachery. The utter pointlessness of what had happened had turned him into this.

Something deep down, some hidden failsafe which he never knew existed, had snapped inside him. The fuse had blown, the switch had been tripped, and he was totally committed to his task.

He had moved as quietly as possible to his target during darkness and had barely blinked throughout the first night. He inched his way through the pitch-black so as to alert no sentry to his presence. For a man of his size to be so stealthy took vast amounts of physical and mental concentration. By dawn, he was exhausted and crept away to return to his hiding place and await the next nightfall.

He spent the day still and silent inside a small space. His discovery would mean his death, and it wasn't his death he had come for. It was someone else's. Someone very particular.

By nightfall he had rested, rehydrated and eaten. He eased himself silently out of his lair, stretched to relieve the cramp in his muscles, and crept back towards his target for another night of watching.

He didn't care how long it took – he would get what he came for.

Hours passed as he inched his way around the target again, looking for any sign of what he wanted. Movement showed ahead and to his right as a silhouette emerged from the side of the building. He watched as the man relieved himself and wandered back out of sight.

This is where he needed to be.

Five others came out and performed the same ritual over the next few hours, but none of them appeared to be who he wanted.

Shortly before the sun began to show off to his left, a familiar shape emerged and leaned a hand against the wall as he undid his zip.

This was the man's best opportunity to get what he came for.

He crept the first few yards until the stretch of open ground left him exposed, then rose and covered the distance in long, purposeful strides.

The man leaning against the wall heard a noise and began to turn. Too late, and strong hands grabbed at him and covered his mouth. A huge fist drove into his soft belly and forced all the air from his lungs. The shorter man's diaphragm went into spasm, and the characteristic sounds of being winded would have escaped his mouth but for the powerful hand clamped over his face. He pissed the remaining contents of his bladder over his attacker's legs, although neither of them noticed.

Twice more he hit him, each massive blow raising the shorter man off his feet until his knees gave out. Both hands seized him tight around the throat and dragged him quickly away from the building.

When out of sight and shrouded in the safety of the shadows once again, the larger man dropped to the floor and held the other tight. There was no sign that his attack had been noticed, and he felt great satisfaction in what was to come.

Half-carrying and half-dragging the smaller man, he took him to the small jetty away from the building. Seizing him by the windpipe, he thrust him into the cold water, holding him under the surface in spite of the desperate and frantic attempts to escape.

It seemed strange to the big man that a person could take so long to drown. He made sure he was looking straight into his eyes as the kicking and clawing became weak, then feeble, then stopped altogether as the last few bubbles rose from the blank face.

"Thank you, Riley," said Simon as he let the now lifeless body of the traitor float away.

ONCE MORE UNTO THE BEACH

Those who had raised objections to further sea travel were grudgingly loading their equipment back aboard *Hope*, helped by the others, who held no such trepidation. A feeling of resignation at having to brave the water once more mixed with the excitement of being on the move again. To be going somewhere new. All nearby buildings were thoroughly raided for any useful supplies, not that they had much space to store it.

Of all the group, only one remained stubbornly against the idea.

Not even the lure of food would convince him as he whined pitifully from the wooden jetty. Of all the members of their party, he alone was not given a chance to vote on their course, not that it would have made a difference.

In the end, Dan had to climb back over the rail and force their last recalcitrant passenger aboard, receiving a threatening growl as he went to force the issue.

"NO," he snapped, fixing Ash with his best wide-eyed stare and trying his best to retain the Alpha dominance over the dog.

Realising he would not win, the now huge German Shepherd nimbly jumped over the fibreglass bulkhead and immediately lost his footing on the moving deck. Whining again, he put his head down and bolted to the lower decks to find a hiding place where he could be sick in peace. Leah cast a look of silent communication to Dan and followed.

The weather was calmer than when they had sought refuge there the day before, and Dan was certain he wasn't alone in praying that it remained that way.

Everyone settled in to their comfortable spots as they had previously, very few of them relishing the prospect of another nauseating day at sea. Typically, the only people happy to be setting sail again were the self-styled co-captains. Mitch and Neil were up on what they were calling the flight deck, arguing good-naturedly over their pre-sail checklist.

Dan stood back next to Adam and had to allow himself a smile; it was clear that neither really knew much about any of what they were saying, but they seemed to believe that if they delivered their opinions with confidence, then people might believe them. The engine was started and revved before it was throttled back and allowed to warm up. None of the complicated computerised equipment was of any real use because it mostly relied on working satellites, of which Dan doubted there were any still on course and feeding any useful information back to the ground.

The mooring lines were cast off, the bumper things designed to stop the boat hitting the side of the jetty were pulled aboard – fenders someone called them – and *Hope* once again moved off to carry them onwards.

Their return journey to the mouth of the sea was again slow progress as the detritus of human disappearance left obstacles in their path. Inside of twenty minutes, they were facing the open sea. The calm inland waters showed an obvious demarcation as the rolling waves of the Channel promised discomfort or worse. Dan forced himself to think rationally; it was only their collective lack of knowledge which made the water-based part of their journey dangerous. The weather wasn't bad, and it would only take them another day at sea to cut out possibly weeks of uncertain travel by road. His fears that *Hope* would be damaged by the storm had been allayed, as the multimillion-pound yacht showed no signs of being the slightest bit affected by the buffeting she had received.

As Neil pushed forward on the throttle lever, they surged forwards and out of the harbour. The ride became instantly rougher, but despite the held breath of the passengers, it seemed no worse than when they left the English coast twenty-four hours prior. Frayed nerves began to relax, and within minutes, a few of the passengers felt safe enough to come out on deck.

One of these, predictably, was Phil as he made straight for the side to be sick. Dan had to wonder why a man with the worst sensitivity to travel sickness he had ever met had volunteered for first a helicopter-borne escape, and now a cross-continent journey by various forms of vehicle. Putting that out of his mind, he turned back to join Neil at the controls.

Mitch gestured for Dan to take his place and bent to open a small cupboard under the wide dash. Curious, Dan leaned over to see what he was doing. Mitch pulled out a Peli case, found it to contain a flare gun and spares, and put it aside to take with them. What the soldier was more interested in, however, was the high-frequency radio set.

"Must be a backup," Mitch said, correctly assuming that Dan was curious. "These things have all manner of satellite comms, but this good old-fashioned lump doesn't need satellites. Bloody finicky things though."

Dan felt a little callous and selfish as he thought that, as much as a godsend Mitch had been, if he'd have been a Signaller instead of an Infantryman, then the possibilities were much more far-reaching.

"Five hundred kilohertz, old boy!" declared Nail raucously.

"Maybe in your day, you old git," replied Mitch, "but that frequency hasn't been used for years now. We had a set at Richards's camp, but few enough of us knew how to work it. I'll admit I only know the very basics," he said as he tinkered with dials and switches.

Noises came from the mic speaker, high-pitched and full of static, as he moved the controls more with curiosity than purpose.

Dan's mind drifted away, daydreaming of finding others with the same technology. That was what had marked out the last few generations as far more advanced: the ability to communicate over long distances instantaneously.

In the last year and a half, they had only managed to create a short-range radio system, and that had been sketchy at best.

His mind returned to the present, and he realised with a shudder that being on deck in the early morning wind before the sun was fully up had left him with a chill.

"I'll go over the maps again," he said to his companions before sliding down the ladder to go inside.

A few nervous faces looked up as he staggered through the small door into the main cabin before they realised he wasn't coming to shout "abandon ship" or anything similarly terrifying. He saw Leah sitting on one of the lavishly cushioned sofas with her carbine next to her and the massive head of an unhappy dog over her other thigh. He sat next to her and produced a map of the Normandy coastline to find their approximate position. Leah leaned over as far as the miserable Ash would allow.

"So we've just left Cabourg," he said, having assured himself of their position by the road signs while exploring their safe harbour of the previous night. He ran his finger along the coastline, only able to guess at their speed and progress. "Today should take us past Calais, and by tonight we should be inland in Belgium. I hope."

"Easy as that!" she replied with a heavy hint of sarcasm.

He shot her a playful look of annoyance and went to find Marie.

SINKING SHIP

The mood at home had improved very little, with mealtimes being a sombre affair without much talk. Gone were the days of productivity, excitement, and faith in strong leadership.

It was easy for almost everyone to blame Dan and the others for leaving, but a few of the deeper-thinking inhabitants knew that it was because everyone who had stayed behind had given up any hope of prospering.

The realisation of being the last generation of the human race alive had slowly, insidiously, sunk in, and all passion for their ongoing lives had ebbed away.

Still, it was easier to blame Dan.

Some spoke openly of leaving, while others just sat in miserable silence and waited for the pointless end of their existence. Why suffer all of the hardships and the stresses of getting this far only to await an empty life without hope? Was that not the point of survival, to propagate the species?

Even the discovery of Henry's disappearance was met with apathy; when he didn't report for work and couldn't be found, his room had been searched, and the obvious signs of his clothing and belongings missing had led to the conclusion of his leaving with the others.

Many wished they had possessed the courage to do just that, but it was too late now.

Their leadership was weak and ill-prepared. Steve was still in a coma – as had become common knowledge after rumours of his death had spread – and everyone just felt like there was no point in getting up tomorrow.

Talk of another migration, of a group who now wished to follow the others, died away as they realised they did not have the knowledge, skills or experience to track them down.

That ship had, quite literally, sailed.

SLOW PROGRESS

Dan had woefully underestimated how quickly they would get into the heart of the continent. That said, it wasn't as though he had made all of the plans in isolation; none of them realised how difficult it would be without the expertise of the people who used to do this all the time.

A life without services being provided was a hard one.

As he stood on the deck with the sun soaking into his face and arms, making a prickle of sweat appear under his body armour, he marvelled at a number of things in a brief moment of introspection:

He realised just how beautiful the world was when the inhabitants were mostly gone and not fighting each other.

He realised just how easy it was for a bit of sunshine to change everyone's outlook on life.

He realised he didn't have a clue, not in the slightest, how they were going to pull this off.

Still, they would just have to figure it out, he guessed.

Progress east along the northern coast of France had been slow, but slow had felt safe and safe felt just fine by him. The water was, by comparison to what they had experienced so far, calm.

Jack and his fishing rod had made a reappearance, and those who felt better about their seaward journey used the other equipment and joined him. The excitement of the first unexpected catch brought squeals of joy and repulsion as the ugly fish flapped around on the deck.

Jack, as usual generating some awe about his quiet and unassuming wealth of knowledge, made the noises rise a whole octave as he calmly held the fish tight with his foot and ended the struggling with a swift stab of the knife he carried.

As the prospect of fresh fish became a firm reality, all spare hands were now dangling the rods and hand lines into their wake, each hook bearing a weighted lure and the dreams of people eager for real food.

Dan watched on from the upper deck as the thrill pulsated around the gaggle of people at the stern of their boat. If ever the name of their yacht meant anything, it meant it right then.

He flicked his cigarette far out over the side as he turned back to Neil, who was sitting comfortably as he piloted the craft gently along the water. Land showed to their right, not close enough to be in great detail but close enough to run to for cover should the weather show any sign of flexing its muscles again.

Dan allowed his worries to abate slightly. They may already be a few days behind the schedule he had in his mind, but that was OK.

They were safe, they were happy, they had hope, and tonight – if the sounds from the lower deck were anything to go by – they would be eating fresh fish.

Land showed ahead of them, indicating their need to head north for a time to stick to the seas and not follow the river into Rouen. Dan chuckled as Neil recited some line from a film about being on "the road to Rouen".

Predictable, but always a happy distraction, Neil's quips were as much a part of their glue, their safety and security as Dan's guns were.

The sun rose to its highest point and began to fall away, still bathing them with warmth despite the briefest of rain showers in the afternoon. A few people panicked that they would be put through the rigors of another storm, but soon relaxed when the sea failed to boil up and throw them around.

By late afternoon, the tub on the lower deck held an assortment of fish, much to the disgust of Marie, who couldn't even stomach the smell of them uncooked, and Dan took the boat closer to the shoreline, as he planned to put in for the night before they reached the built-up areas of Boulogne and Calais. Avoiding the larger population centres was a cautious move, and one based on some hard-earned experience in their past. Stick to the quieter places and reduce the chances of a confrontation. Mindful that anyone they encountered would likely be settled and well resourced – much as they had been at home – and that they were the nomads kept him wary of outside contact.

A wide estuary opened up ahead of them as Dan allowed Mitch to take back the helm. He did so with satirical ceremony as he placed the captain's hat back on his head. With a smile, Dan sat next to him and lit another cigarette, his enjoyment of the moment only slightly marred by their need to find safe shelter before dark.

As the land encroached either side of them, Mitch slowed their progress in order to navigate the long, ponderous sandbanks sweeping inwards between the two banks of the river mouth. Slowly, they headed inland, this time without the obstacles of anchored wreckage as they had encountered the previous day.

The wide, shallow inlet flowed lazily towards buildings in the distance. Almost half a mile ensued before a mooring appeared ahead.

"Bring her in to the left," said Dan, pointing.

"Port," replied Mitch.

Dan shot him a quizzical look.

"You have to say port for this side," he gestured to his left, "and starboard for that side," he said, gesturing to his right.

Dan paused, unsure whether he has walking into a joke or not. "Well, Captain," he said with a small bow dripping with sarcasm, "kindly take us in to the port side."

Mitch smirked from one side of his mouth, happy to have corrected someone and not been rebuked.

As the boat slowed, a flash of movement between some buildings launched Dan into a reflex action. As one, the cigarette was thrown away and carbine swung from his back in practised hands to point towards the source of his sudden wariness.

Never, not since they had been attacked by a pack of dogs, had he ever let his instincts be ignored.

"Go past, don't stop," he said in a low voice, his eye pressed into the scope.

Mitch applied more power to the engines and veered their course to starboard as he also kept one eye on the buildings. Neil had responded to Dan's reaction immediately and climbed down the ladder to hiss at the gathered people on the lower deck to get inside and stay quiet.

They moved, silent and obedient, towards the relative safety of the cabin. Leah and Adam emerged, readying weapons as they came. The young girl shimmied effortlessly to the upper deck and asked quietly for a report.

"Movement between the buildings. Could be nothing," Dan said succinctly.

Leah knew that it may well be nothing, but she also knew that they hadn't survived as long as they had by not being careful. She turned and looked down to Adam, nodding towards the buildings now shrinking behind them. He crouched by the low bulkhead and watched over the barrel of his rifle.

Now out of sight, Dan relaxed from squinting down the optic and asked Mitch to turn them around.

"Big lazy circle like we don't have a care in the world," he said softly before turning to Neil and nodding aft for him to join Adam. He caught Leah's eye and pointed her to the prow.

Mitch did as was expected and turned the boat in a long, looping manoeuvre before aiming it back towards the small wooden dock.

Five pairs of eyes watched like hawks for signs of anything amiss, four of those over the sights of weapons. Dan couldn't quite place it yet, but there was something definitely wrong about the place; it was not just that he had thought he'd seen something or someone, but his skin tingled with a familiar sense of being uncomfortable with the mental picture of the dock, and knowing that meant his brain probably hadn't connected the dots yet.

He scanned every inch of the dockside through his scope, trying to figure out what it was that was making him so edgy.

It began to dawn on him that the area didn't have the look or feel of a place abandoned long ago, but more that it still held a type of function, like it still lived.

As this realisation hit him, Leah called out from where she lay on the prow.

"Go! Go!" she bawled, sounding desperate.

As Mitch opened the throttle up wide and launched the pointed prow of *Hope* high on the water, a single shot rang out. The sound of hundreds of tiny projectiles hitting the fibreglass echoed like a sudden hailstorm of lead.

Luckily, the shot was small and the distance too great to do any real damage, but their fear was palpable at the sudden savagery of the noise. Dan heard screams from below decks as he fought desperately to hang onto the guardrail and stay upright, such was the aggressiveness of the acceleration. Mitch stayed at near full power for only a few more seconds, but that was sufficient to move them well away from any following fire. As he slowed to a more sensible speed, Dan gave him further instructions.

"Stick to the middle of the channel," Dan said as he stood tall to see Leah at the very front of the boat. Their sudden flight had thrown her back, and Dan saw her on her knees rubbing the back of her head. She noticed her audience and made her way back to him unsteadily, protesting that it was nothing. He ignored her transparency and felt her head, prompting a pained gasp when he touched the sore patch on the back of her skull, which was already swelling.

"Get below and get something cold on it," he said, expecting her to argue and have to be told again. She said nothing and made slow progress inside.

Neil and Adam had regained their composure after being similarly sprawled across the deck when they fled, but they were unhurt. Dan followed Leah inside to find the cabin in complete disarray; his dog was howling from fear and feeling wretched at not being on dry land.

Equipment was everywhere, as were the tangles of people who had been caught unaware by the powerful surge in movement.

A dozen questions were fired in his direction at once and he held up his hands to ward off the onslaught.

"Someone took a cheap shot at us from the docks, that's all," he said smoothly, continuing before anyone asked another. "Is everyone OK?" he asked, looking around. He saw Marie and Sera by Ash, the former rummaging in a bag of her equipment. He saw others dusting themselves off after being thrown around, but nothing seemed overly tragic. His eyes rested on Kate, who was holding Leah firmly by the head and looking into her eyes.

Kate had that look in her eye that took over her whole expression when she worked on someone, and that worried Dan.

He reached them just as a small light was being shone at Leah's pupils. Kate held a finger up directly in front of the girl and told her to follow it. Leah did as she was told and he sensed Kate relax slightly. Over the noise of the others disentangling and Jack's expressive language, he asked his miniature assassin again if she was all right.

"Hurts," she said, screwing her eyes up, "a lot."

Dan suspected there may have even been a tear coming from one of her eyes, but reckoned that a nasty bang to the head was probably one of the few things which could illicit such a response from her. Leaving her in Kate's capable hands, he went back outside.

Hoping to figure out what the hell to do now.

ALL AT SEA

"Well, we can't stay here," said Mitch. "No idea if they were on their own or if they have boats or anything. It's pretty clear they don't want us visiting."

Dan agreed, looking around at the assembled faces. Marie, Kate, Neil, Mitch, Jack and himself huddled in a small circle on the upper deck of the *Hope*. Leah was inside, relieved of her equipment on Kate's strict instructions – although Dan doubted she was still totally unarmed – and lying flat, being kept watch on by Sera with the recently sedated dog lying flat against her, snoring loudly.

"Well, we can't go out to sea without any working radar equipment or anything," said Neil. "That's just asking for trouble."

"Options?" said Marie, fractionally before Dan could utter one of his trademark lines. A small smirk to herself told him that she knew exactly what she had done, and the slightly bewildered look on his face let her know that her timing had been impeccable.

"We'll have to anchor up in the bay for the night," said Jack.

They all looked at him.

"Well, we can't go inland past where we were attacked now, and who's to say we'll find anywhere safer there anyhow," he said, answering their blank looks. "Plus, as Neil rightly says, we can't go back into the sea this time of day. We've got maybe an hour of daylight left at best, and that's not enough to guarantee finding another safe harbour."

Nobody had a rebuttal, and nobody offered a better solution.

"Three-hour shifts, two on at a time, though. Mitch, can you take second watch with Adam?" Dan asked.

Mitch nodded his agreement.

"Jack, can you take first watch with Neil, please?" he asked the older man.

"Of course I can," Jack replied, almost sounding affronted at the possibility that he wouldn't be asked. "I'll get some things and be back." He left without a word.

Mitch and Neil began discussing where to drop anchor, inevitably turning it into a heated debate, so Dan led the two women down the ladder to talk further.

"As Leah's out for the day, I'll need a volunteer to work the last shift with me from three a.m. until six, so it'll be a long day for them tomorrow," he said to them. He didn't expect Marie to volunteer, even though she hadn't once claimed pregnancy to avoid any hardship, but because she simply wasn't one of those people who could operate without sleep.

"She may be out tomorrow too," said Kate reprovingly, ever implying that he worked the girl too hard.

A loud noise interrupted their discussion as the loud chorus of the prow anchor chain falling away overtook all other sounds. It stopped quickly, betraying the shallow depth of the small inlet, and began to slowly swing the boat around so that the nose pointed into the flow of the tide, like a compass finding true north.

"Ask carefully," said Marie when she could hear her voice again, "because some people in there will say yes to anything you want. Now come and eat something before you get some sleep."

He followed her back to the main cabin as Jack emerged, ready for an exposed few hours. He had a large pump-action shotgun slung over his back, offered a grizzly nod, and climbed the steps to the argument pit that was the flight deck.

Dan checked in on Leah and Ash, finding both well cared for and not wanting to disturb them. Looking around the room, he wondered who to choose as his backup during the dead hours before dawn – always the hardest shift of the night.

Sera and Kate were caring for the injured and unwell – his adopted daughter and his dog primarily, along with the ever travel-sick Phil, who now looked very pale and dehydrated.

Marie was not an option for night duty, nor were Pip or Ana. Lou and Laura had become the worker bees inside the cabin, making sure everyone was fed and watered.

His eyes rested on Henry, who was sitting apart from the others and trying his hardest not to be caught staring at Dan with a devotion which would embarrass Ash if he were conscious.

No, not Henry. He would want to talk all night, and that would be worse than sitting on deck alone. Jimmy was his obvious choice, but since setting sail two days ago, he had been very quiet and withdrawn, no doubt suffering badly with being on the water for the first time in his life.

Another face sat apart, peering through glasses at a small paper-back book she had found aboard. Suddenly aware that she was the subject of scrutiny from another human being, she almost dropped the book in panic.

Some time ago, he remembered her admitting that she loved the lab work because she didn't have to speak to many people. He understood that, but he also knew that there was always a time to be outside of your comfort zone. He moved over to her, seeing her shrink in size and almost try to get in the book without appearing overtly rude.

"Relax, Emma," he said, "I need your help."

"Me?" she asked, wide-eyed. "What can I do?"

"Set an alarm for three a.m. and sit on deck with me until sunrise," he said simply.

Her already wide eyes grew even larger, as she wouldn't have thought to make any connection between herself and sentry duty.

Dan stifled a laugh at her reaction.

"Last watch of the night, because Leah's hurt and I need someone with sharp senses to keep me awake. It's not a date," he said with a smile, "and bring your gun," he added.

Bewildered and flattered that she had been asked, she nodded and started to press the buttons on her digital watch as instructed.

He ate beans and sausages cold from the tin before cuddling up with Marie in one of the bedrooms for a few hours' sleep inside the lurching, cramped space.

Luxurious as the *Hope* was, he doubted it was designed for so many people and a dog to live on board for any length of time.

The night passed restlessly; most people were in more of a state of semiconsciousness or light hibernation than actual sleep.

At two fifty-five in the morning, Dan's watch began a high-pitched beep which earned him a sudden and sharp elbow in the ribs from Marie.

He climbed over her to extract himself from the bed, earning more grumbling from her, and slipped into his vest before picking up his carbine. He closed the door as silently as possible and crept outside to find Emma waiting by the doorway wearing her own body armour with the gun on her chest.

She hadn't brought any extra clothing, it seemed, so Dan picked up one of the blankets stored in a tub on deck for when the rich former owners felt a chill and sent one of the crew to fetch something for them.

They climbed the ladder, nodding to Adam and Mitch and receiving a muttered report of no activity. They switched places with the two men and settled into the warm seats at the controls. A small camp cooker had been set up with a large bottle of water, two cups, and the obligatory jar of instant coffee. Dan set the burner going to heat the two cups' worth of water he poured in.

Not a word passed between them until the coffee was made, and even then it was only politeness in her thanking him which broke the silence.

That was another reason for picking her.

Only when the tide turned and the boat first went slack on the anchor chain and then turned ponderously around to face the prow where the stern had been did she say anything.

Her sudden panic had elicited a small laugh from Dan, unfairly, as he wouldn't have known about what would happen either if Jack hadn't warned him to expect it in the early hours. Before he could explain it, she understood that she was experiencing the changing tide and settled down. He liked that about her: her analytical mind and sharp intelligence only complemented her lack of social comfort around others. She was actually very easy company.

They sat on deck, Dan in short sleeves and his heavy vest and Emma feeling the chilly breeze far more and wrapped up in a blanket, enjoying the comfortable silence and waiting for the dawn.

UNEXPECTED ARRIVALS

The last thing anyone would have expected was for a pair of new additions to arrive.

Two men, both dishevelled, seemed to have been travelling for a while when they wandered up to the gardens on foot overloaded with whatever belongings they could carry.

Although one was armed with a hunting rifle, neither seemed the slightest bit hostile. Still, their unannounced arrival at the gardens elicited a flurry of activity and not less than a few screams of terror.

They were no threat to them; they were dehydrated and exhausted. They were taken into the cool, given chilled water to drink, and fed fresh bread and salad.

The two bearded men ate as though they had never tasted such ambrosia before. They ate until their shrunken stomachs filled, and the pleasure of the food became sudden discomfort.

Maggie was reminded of footage she had seen of prisoners of war being released into the care of their fellow countrymen, of their thin frames and looks of emptiness.

Quietly, she sent Cedric away to call Lexi from the "big house," as they called it, to inspect and vet these strangers.

They sat, full to the brim on very little food and water, almost comatose as the nutrients washed into their bodies. They could barely contain their gratitude; one of them broke down in tears at their kindness. It was as though they had been walking through hell – it was almost hot enough that summer – and had just reached an oasis.

Maggie accepted their thanks humbly, as was her manner, and returned to the doorway of the room in time to see Dan's – no, Lexi's –Discovery fly down the small ramp into the courtyard. She slid lithely from behind the wheel, followed by the muscular and intimidating Paul from the passenger side.

"Where are they?" she snapped at the older woman. Maggie didn't appreciate her tone; Dan always showed respect and deference to her and Cedric, even when the situation was dangerous. This upstart had a lot of growing to do before she could hope to fill his absent shoes. Still, Maggie shook away the negativity and answered her kindly.

"In the office," she said, and turned and walked as Lexi fell in step beside her. "They wandered in half an hour ago; both are dehydrated and exhausted. They've been carrying everything they could salvage from their vehicle after it broke down this morning. They've been walking ever since. I don't think they are a danger," she added finally, making her opinion clear.

"We'll see," replied Lexi sullenly as she snatched up the hunting rifle they had carried and inspected it before thrusting it at Paul.

In truth, her attitude wasn't intended to be obnoxious, but was coming across that way out of fear. Dan's easy manner when gently interrogating newcomers was a talent, not a matter of training. He had looked so many good and bad people in the eyes that he just seemed to have a sixth sense about who to trust. She saw none of that skill in herself, so fell back on being the militant to be safe.

The arrival of two armed people dressed all in black woke the two men slightly, sobering them from their blissful state of being fed and safe. They nervously sat up and waited for instruction from the woman in front of them who seemed barely able to contain her hostility.

"I'm going to search your kit. Do you have any other weapons than the rifle?" she snapped.

"No," stammered one of the men, seemingly more alert than the other. His voice croaked and cracked, so he tried again. "No. Only a couple of sharp knives for food. We avoid trouble; the rifle is for hunting rabbits," he said, trying to show as much deference as he could to appease the angry woman.

Lexi said nothing and strode outside, dragging the two large backpacks. She upended the bags and regarded the contents strewn across the ground, sifting through them with her foot as she pulled a face at the smell.

She went back inside, having done nothing to search their belongings effectively other than to display her power like a dominant ape.

"Names," she ordered them.

"I'm Ben," said the alert one, and indicated at the half-asleep man next to him, "that's Will. We're brothers."

Lexi said nothing in response, merely looked around for Matty. Finding him, she gave instructions for them to be brought back to the house and cleaned up before being told to wait in the dining room.

"I'll leave Paul with you to make sure everyone is safe," she added as she strode to her vehicle to assemble the council. "And don't let them out of your sight," she warned her partner as she climbed behind the wheel.

Ben and Will laughed as they enjoyed their first hot showers in as long as they could recall. Paul had sent Matty back to the gardens, embarrassed over Lexi's behaviour, and he didn't want to be forced into a discussion about it. He knew that her rudeness was due to her own insecurity, and that Dan's easy manner was born of a confidence in being the most dangerous person in the room. Usually.

Paul listened to the two young men who, now clean and beardless, appeared to be in their early twenties. Their back-and-forth repartee was amusing, and Paul guessed they had bickered and mocked each other in such a loving way since they could walk. He liked them, and he knew nothing about them yet.

"Come on, lads. Speed it up, please!" he said to them when there was more banter than washing going on. They reluctantly dried themselves off, laughing at their pale chins and cheeks, as they had been sunburned before they had shaved, and dressed in the comfortable grey prison tracksuits that always seemed to be given to the newest arrivals.

Giggling quietly between themselves, they followed Paul downstairs and into the dining hall. Cara had supplied a small snack buffet as she liked to do with all newcomers, although she hadn't had much opportunity recently. The two men looked between Cara and Paul for permission, and when nodded towards the food, they flew in to gorge themselves. They clearly hadn't eaten properly for a long time. Noises of childlike joy escaped from one as he found a small tray of puff pastry sweet treats, holding one aloft as though he were blessing his brother with a holy relic. Their joy was infectious, but both Cara's and Paul's amusement at their happiness was stifled when the door opened and the council members entered.

Cara became sensible and sat down at her usual place at the larger table, and she was joined by Lexi, Lizzie, Andrew and Mike.

Paul went to take his leave until Lexi ordered him to stay.

"No, keep an eye on them," she said, simultaneously embarrassing him again and making herself look overly churlish.

Paul held his tongue. Her attempts at trying to let everyone know she had power were starting to wear thin on him already.

"Welcome!" exclaimed Mike to the nervous subjects of discussion. "I hope you're feeling better now for being clean and eating."

Ben paused with a pastry halfway in his mouth and was torn between taking it out or finishing the action. Having been raised not to show people the contents of your mouth at the dinner table, he bit down on it and chewed. He looked at his brother for any kind of backup, but it seemed that Will was content to let Ben do all the talking.

Painfully slowly, he chewed until he could force the pastry down in one uncomfortable swallow. Unfortunately, this forced him to require a drink to wash it down and prevent him choking, resulting in twenty seconds of very awkward silence until he finally answered Mike's question.

"Yes. Thank you," he said lamely, completely undermining the gravity of the time it took him to think of what to say.

The assembled faces allowed themselves to crack into smiles at the stupidity of the exchange, all except Lexi, who scowled at them.

Their story emerged, haltingly, having to be extracted piecemeal at times. They were brothers. Will was at university in York and Ben worked in an office in Leeds. When it happened, Will told Ben to stay put and that he was coming to get him. They had wandered from place to place ever since, caching supplies and moving on whenever other people threatened their safety. They had no real purpose or aim; they were just waiting to be told what to do by someone. A few tales of hiding and running away from gangs were told, and after the first winter, they decided to stay away from towns and wander the rural places instead. That's where they found the rifle.

"So you've just been moving from house to house, living off what you could find for all this time?" asked Lizzie.

The two men looked at each other, as though they had one collective mind. "Yeah," they chorused.

Almost stunned by their apparent simplicity, Mike moved on to the subject of them staying.

Again, their trademark eye contact followed by another affirmative chorus.

"So what can you do?" said Lexi quietly, trying to mimic Dan's presence when he spoke softly but everyone realised he was angry.

"We both climb; we're good at that," said Will.

"I meant what can you do to help around here?" she replied coolly. "What use are you?"

Grasping the meaning of the only person who didn't seem to want them there, Will thought before answering in a measured voice. "We've survived for over a year. We've been chased, hunted, but never found. We can get in and out of places and people don't even know we've been there. We've stolen supplies right out of the pockets of the people who were looking to take ours. So that's what we can do. If you need scouts, we can do that."

He sat back, pleased with his speech, and surveyed the room.

They were all convinced, all except the one with the gun on her chest.

"Thank you, both," said Mike. "Paul, could you please show them into the lounge? I'm sure they don't need to be watched anymore."

Paul nodded his head for them to follow, which they did, taking as much of the food in front of them as they could manage. Will looked back and smiled as best as he could with his arms full and a plastic cup held in his teeth.

The door closed.

Mike turned to Lexi. "You said you needed two new Rangers. There they are," he said.

The murmurs of agreement from all the others made her almost burst with rage.

"We don't know them! At all!" she exclaimed loudly. "They could be anyone from anywhere, have you considered that? What if they are from another group and want inside knowledge on how to take this place?" She stood as she tried to make the others see reason.

"I'm sure we're past all that kind of thing by now," Mike said dismissively.

In truth, her protestations would have been better received if she hadn't become a brooding, angry woman who seemed desperate to stamp her authority. She had cried wolf, and now the others wouldn't listen to her.

"I'm telling you all right now this is a bad idea, and I don't trust them," she said, getting up and leaving the room.

TEMPORARY SANCTUARY

After a rough night spent anchored in the centre of the wide inlet, almost everyone was feeling some ill effect at being sleep-deprived and nauseous.

Dan had roused the group as the sun rose, breakfast was eaten, and they were underway before the glowing orb was fully visible on the horizon.

Very little talking and even less laughter was heard; they had all been worn out by the last few days. Dan knew they needed to get to land and regroup. He had checked on his teenage ninja first thing, finding her stiff, as the pain had travelled from her head to her neck. Kate had dosed her up well enough but firmly declared that she wasn't fit for duty for a week. Both Dan and Leah took that to mean a couple of days at the most, but he carefully avoided any mention of an early recovery and told the girl to rest. Ash still snored against her leg, the sedative having worked well.

He climbed to the flight deck and asked his co-captains to take them out. For the second time they didn't expect, they were going back out to sea. Hopefully for the last time.

Sailing towards the rising sun, they had to turn slightly north to get around the headland as they passed the bigger French coastal towns. Soon, land became visible in the far distance to their port side, the iconic slash of white belonging to the Dover cliffs sparking mixed emotions in many. Dan wondered if he declared that they had had enough fun and were going home, just how many would be happy with that.

He pushed it from his mind as the sea walls of Calais ferry port came into view. Cruising past, they saw a similar sight to the other large ports, with huge vessels slowly dying of neglect. He thought that the docks would be a goldmine for scavenging but could not afford the risks or the delay. Another hour saw them further along the coast and out of French waters. As Bruges approached, Dan consulted the map feverishly with Mitch to be sure they were planning to turn inland at the best place.

"I say we do it," he said to the soldier. "Go inland here to Antwerp."

"Sounds good to me!" replied Mitch.

NO CHANGE

Lizzie had been forced to resort to placing a feeding tube into Steve's nose and down into his stomach. He'd been out too long to be without sustenance now, and she was painfully reminded of having to care for the terminally ill and elderly in her previous life.

Steve's perpetual state of unconsciousness was becoming a worry to everyone. It had been almost a week and he hadn't moved at all. She could still see no obvious reason for it. The head injury hadn't seemed catastrophic; in fact, she doubted whether it had fractured his skull much at all. The internal bleeding hadn't spread, as there was no swelling or livid bruising, plus if it had, she reasoned that he would probably be dead by now. The leg looked gruesome, but should heal.

She wasn't so ignorant to what was happening to the group, despite spending nearly all her time in medical. She had checked out the two new arrivals. The two young men were declared to be in good physical condition despite being told they were found close to death from dehydration. Although the two were a couple of years apart in age, they were so similar that they could have passed for twins. The older of the two seemed to be their joint spokesperson, which she found odd, but she took their medical histories and gave them the stamp of approval.

Some disagreement between other council members left the question of their employment up in the air. It seemed that Lexi didn't want them and was happy to try and half train some sort of militia to be called on at times of need. None of the candidates were particularly enthusiastic about it.

Andrew had employed the two under the umbrella of Logistics to be scouts, and orders were given that they be armed from their healthy stock of weaponry. The two now moved freely among the whole group, weapons on their hips, and were the cause of much excitement. Nobody new had been seen in a while.

She was too busy, too distracted, to think any more on their arrival and appointments.

When – if – Steve woke up, then he would surely know what to do with them and Lexi.

If.

WHERE IS BELGIUM, ANYWAY?

Leah's question had many answers to it, some of those now utterly irrelevant.

"It's a small country between France and the Netherlands where the European Union used to be," Dan answered, hoping not to prompt too many follow-up questions from her.

"OK," she said, obviously thinking, "but what do they do there?"

Neil stepped in to help, speaking from behind the controls of the boat. "They make beer, chocolate and waffles and have a very clean subway system," he said.

"And it's where people like to sign peace treaties and stuff," added Mitch.

Leah thought about this for a moment. "Sounds... nice," she said with her trademark inflection of cutting sarcasm before climbing back down to go back inside. She had been allowed to move to get some fresh air but was still obviously suffering some from the heavy blow to her head.

Dan was under strict orders from Kate that she wasn't allowed out to play for another couple of days. Having never seen her subdued like she was, he planned to let her recover properly.

Following the land on their right, they left the Channel and followed an endless series of twists and turns as the inlet wound its ponderous way to the open water. Sticking to the centre of the wide stretch after their most recent experience of the continental survivors, they sailed serenely into the heart of Belgium as they avoided similar debris to what they had experienced in France.

By late afternoon, they were flanked on both sides by massive industrial docklands. A never-ending mass of concrete in every direction suddenly opened up to open areas of grass before industry closed in on them again.

Betraying his nervousness, Dan checked a map over and over until he called his opinion to Neil and Mitch.

"I reckon Antwerp will be about a mile ahead around the next bend," he said, without his normal air of confidence. A sheltered port to their right, home to some slowly eroding fishing boats, caught his eye. "How about we swing over there and check that place out?"

Without acknowledgement, the boat swung to starboard, cautiously heading into the sheltered bay where a few trawlers sat abandoned. Dan pointed to an empty spot on a jetty with a long walkway leading to land. Mitch brought her in gently as Adam and Dan jumped ashore to secure *Hope* to the moorings.

Guns up, Dan and Adam stalked forward followed by Mitch. Dan would have felt more comfortable being backed up by a dog and a child; it was not that he didn't have faith in the others, but more that he felt most secure with Leah and Ash, but as both of them were out of play, he had to have trust in others.

Dan made solid ground and went to one knee. Mitch fanned out to his left, pointing Adam to go right. Quickly, thoroughly and efficiently, they cleared the immediate surroundings of the dockyard and found nothing to suggest that anyone had been there for months. A green film covered all of the boats on dry land, with obvious signs of neglect everywhere. The three men regrouped and were joined by Neil, having instructed everyone else to stay on the boat. A glance back at the *Hope* showed a grumpy-looking Irishman standing staunch on the deck with his shotgun.

"Area looks clear," said Dan to his almost entire military force. "Mitch, Adam, clear that building," he said, indicating a large single-storey industrial unit. "Neil, with me." He set off, flanked by the older man and intentionally setting a slower pace than he would have for his teenage assassin.

They cleared the perimeter, finding that they had been very fortunate in randomly choosing a secure compound to moor up in. Relaxing slightly, Dan went back to find the big building was an almost empty hangar. He deployed the other two to clear the three remaining buildings to their left while he and Neil cleared the two to the right.

When they all returned to report no signs of life, he lowered his carbine and took a full 360 perspective.

They were now the proud owners of their own fenced compound near Antwerp. Their incursion into the continent had been almost entirely unobstructed and unchallenged in the grand scheme of things. They had safely crossed the Channel.

The realisation hit Dan like a crashing wave and threatened to invoke something resembling feelings deep inside him. He had to force himself to remain calm and not fall to the earth, realising that the crossing had been far more dangerous than anyone had anticipated.

Now to business.

"Neil, get everyone off and into that building," he said, indicating the single-storey warehouse which stood closest to the jetty. "When everyone is off, strip the boat of everything and start pumping the diesel into the jerrycans." He turned to Mitch and Adam. "Go around the perimeter again and check for any vehicles inside this compound. After that, get the bikes ashore."

He turned away to look inland as the men scurried away to their tasks. He heard shouts behind him as the orders to disembark for the final time were given. He even fancied he heard a shout of celebration to mark the end of their water adventures for the foreseeable future; he had to admit he felt the same.

They were in Europe, safely on the continent, and now they had to scavenge like experts.

DIFFERENCE OF OPINION

"No, it's decided," said Mike, holding up one hand to staunch Lexi's flow of objections. "The lads will go and clear the place, then call in the Logistics team to fill up the wagons."

She stood, fighting to contain her fury, and left the room.

Always, it had been the job of the Rangers to clear and search a location before Logistics cleared it. Always. Now, it seemed, because she objected to the appointment of two people she didn't trust, they had completely circumvented her authority and armed them anyway. They were what? Logistic Rangers?

It was bullshit, she told them it was bullshit, and she was ignored.

She stormed into Ops, startling Rich, and fumed at him that Dan would never have been ignored like they had just done to her. If he had raised objections to anything, then she was pretty damn sure that he would be listened to and obeyed.

"I mean, he dragged someone out of here who he said was a bloody paedophile and he was never seen again!" she raged at the bewildered Marine. "Who questioned his authority then? Nobody."

Rich averted his eyes in case he gave away some small notion that he had been totally complicit in the murder of said paedophile. Having heard the confessions himself, he had no doubt as to the man's guilt. But still, they did just kill him on Dan's say-so.

Luckily, Lexi was too angry to notice Rich's expression and had carried on ranting.

"This is just what Penny tried to do ages ago; the Rangers are being cut out by the others because they don't like the answer they were given." She stopped and stared at him, waiting for an answer or some form of communication other than a blank look.

She received nothing.

"Fuck this," she said, throwing her arms in the air before storming out of the office.

"Wait," Rich said, investing the word with every bit of authority he used to possess. It was a voice which had cut through battlefields, which tore through recruits and silenced parade squares. It was the voice of a Royal Marine Corporal, and it stopped Lexi in her tracks.

She turned back to him, stunned.

"If you have a problem, then go and fix it. Don't stand here bitching about what Dan would've done; go and do it yourself. You want people to respect your authority? Then earn that respect."

With that, he turned away and left her open-mouthed in the doorway. He was right, of course. She knew she was acting the brat when she should have been emulating that calm authority which she missed so much.

She closed her mouth, turned back towards the dining room and strode in ready to tell them all what she thought.

DRY LAND

"I'm sure you'll all be sad to abandon the boat," Dan said to the group as they shuffled close to him, interrupting their business in preparing the warehouse for a brief stay.

"Abandon *Hope* all ye who enter here!" declared Neil in his best Shakespearean voice.

Silence shrouded the whole group as he realised the carelessness in his words.

"Get it? Abandon? Hope?" he tried with a smile, desperately attempting to rescue the joke. "No?" He hung his head and muttered, "Tough crowd."

"No," said Dan sarcastically, turning back to the others. "Anyway… We've got a secure compound here which we'll use as a base for a few days to gather supplies and look for vehicles. Marie will sort out the tasks, and Neil will organise the rotas for keeping watch. Me and a couple of others will be making runs starting tomorrow to see what we can find." He looked around the assembled faces. No questions arose. "Ladies and gentlemen, Bienvenue en Belgique!" he said loudly and in a terrible accent.

Not all of the group understood, but still a ragged cheer of success rippled around their temporary home. Dan jumped down from his podium and beamed at his group. Truth was, he was happy to have made it here. He scanned the room, his eyes falling on the temporarily fallen and debilitated from their sea crossing.

Ash was groggy and weak from barely eating for three days, Leah lay propped up half-asleep from her concussion, and Phil was curled up in a foetal position after a few days of being constantly sick, with Jimmy beside him looking no better. Despite the losses, which he assured himself weren't permanent, they had left their island and got to the continent without tragedy and in some semblance of working order. He called that a win.

Predictably, Henry hovered with a cup of coffee for him which he accepted with as brief a thanks as was polite. The boy was starting to get on his nerves with his idolism. He was well built and strong for his age, but there was such an immaturity to him that it irked Dan. Thirteen-year-old Leah was more sensible and switched-on than most adults, so maybe he thought her achievements were making him judge the boy more harshly.

No. There was no room for tourists or baggage on this trip, and the lad had chosen to come despite being told he couldn't. Dan would have to have a word in private with him soon and lay out his responsibilities very plainly.

Food was prepared, supplies were stacked and inventoried, the guard was set and they were safe on dry land. Dan finally allowed himself to relax.

He wandered through the group, talking to people as he wound his way among them, aiming for Leah. When he reached her, his heart sank. She did not look well. Her pale skin prickled with sweat and her eyes were closed tightly. She was surrounded by Marie, Kate and Sera, all of whom were tending to her in different ways. It was evident how badly the blow to the head had affected her. Sensing his own discomfort, Ash whined pitifully and pushed his huge head in between the women to nuzzle at the girl.

Dan saw a spark of her personality shine through then; despite the pain she was in, she still managed a crooked half-smile as she told the worried dog she had no food for him. He would've spoken to her, laid a reassuring hand on her shoulder or something to try and comfort her, only there was no room around her.

Instead, he reverted to the only other way he knew to fix a problem: direct action. His mind was made up as soon as he had seen her. As a group, they were in pretty rough shape after the last few days, and progress would just have to wait until they were all fully fit.

Snapping his fingers to summon Ash, he turned on his heel and walked speedily for the exit, almost knocking a grinning Henry to the floor, who was standing so close, and spilling the remaining coffee down both of them. Dan's temper, affected by lack of sleep and worry for Leah, finally broke.

He swore loudly at the boy, shoving him in the chest and sending him sprawling backwards as he threw down the tin cup in a frustrated tantrum.

"Every bloody time I turn around, you're in my face!" he yelled at him, too stressed and angry to realise he was terrifying him and others around them. As suddenly as the fury was on him, it evaporated, leaving only the hollow emptiness of unnecessary anger behind. Too tired to explain or apologise, he stepped around his unfortunate victim and left the building.

Stomping away to the jetty where the *Hope* was moored, he sat and dangled his feet from the walkway as he smoked. Ash lay down and watched him from as close as he could get while still remaining firmly on dry land.

Dan felt bad for his outburst. He felt bad for scaring the boy; as annoying as Henry could be, he didn't deserve what had just happened. He reflected on the advice he had been given about bullies when he was a child and about the advice he had given schoolchildren when he had cause to speak to them as a police officer.

The concept of a bully acting out because of their own fear and insecurity was suddenly so apparently true to him that it almost hurt.

His miserable introspection was halted as Neil approached. Dan had no doubt that he had seen the incident inside but couldn't bring himself to raise the subject out of embarrassment.

With a symphony of groans and cracking joints, Neil lowered himself to sit beside Dan. Silence hung for a few beats, no doubt as Neil decided the best way to say what he had come to say.

"I'm guessing we'll want to stay here for a few days until everyone settles?" he said, reading Dan's transparent thoughts.

"Yes," Dan replied, staring into the green, scummy water of rocky shallows beneath his feet. "Double-check the perimeter is secure, twenty-four-seven lookouts. We'll start ranging on the bikes tomorrow in pairs to find supplies and vehicles. Three, four days tops?"

Neil nodded, and for once had nothing more to say. He stayed where he was for a moment, no doubt dreading the return journey to his feet after feeling how stiff and sore the journey had made his body feel so far. Eventually, and with just as much noise, he got back up and walked back to the building, telling Dan over his shoulder that he'd get Mitch and Adam to do the perimeter.

Dan sat in silence for a while until his restless dog started making noises from the artificial shore. Flicking away the end of his cigarette, he climbed back to his feet and set about the job of securing their small fishing compound and making it defensible during their stay.

As Mitch and Adam went along the fence line meticulously looking for signs of weakness or damage, Dan set about some temporary top cover. Scanning the skyline in their small corner of home, he only saw two places where the height advantage would be sufficient to see all around them. The roof of a building didn't fill him with confidence, as he doubted it would sustain anyone's weight, especially after months of neglect.

The other option might have turned the stomachs of some, however. The biggest of the fishing boats moored in their man-made harbour had a large centre mast with a crow's nest at the very top. It was the best vantage point for hundreds of yards in any direction, and someone up there with a rifle could protect them easily. Despite Dan's healthy respect for gravity and his dislike at being too far off the ground, he climbed the welded steel rungs of the ladder to reach the top. Luckily, the size of the boat made it feel far sturdier in the water, and it wallowed and pitched far less than their yacht did. Breathing heavily, he made it through the opening and into the wide metal basket. Trying not to look down, he used the scope of his carbine to scan the terrain. Satisfied that it was the best option despite the difficulty in reaching it, he ran through plans for manning the nest and what shifts they should take until he could delay no more.

With a resigned sigh, he climbed carefully back down and went to ask Mitch to take over the watch. He happily agreed, too quickly in fact, and interrupted Dan to show him a patch of brown pellets on the dusty ground just outside the fence.

"Deer?" asked Dan, his stomach's thoughts pushing to the head of the queue.

"I reckon so," replied Mitch excitedly.

"Suppressed weapons only," Dan replied. "I don't want to be attracting too much attention if we can avoid it."

Calling everyone back inside, he laid out the plans. Mitch would take shifts in the nest during daylight and others would do night duty; this sentry duty may have to fall to the non-combatants, Dan warned, in order to allow others some much-needed sleep. It wasn't ideal, but it was better than burning out through exhaustion.

Barrels and other obstacles were dragged into positions to allow defensible cover should they need it, and Dan added a word of caution to the group that there were signs of animals around and not to worry if they heard shooting, as it would probably be their dinner. A sudden flash of white met Dan's eyes when he mentioned fresh meat as the faces looking at him broke into smiles. Already a large fire was burning inside a contraption of metal and concrete which Jack had spent hours preparing, and the first gutted fish were being laid onto the mesh as tins were heated alongside them.

The combination of a purpose, some small excitement, and dry land were already having a positive effect on everyone. Dan guessed it was overdue having that discussion with Henry, although now it would have to start with a heartfelt apology.

NEW BLOOD

The twins, as everyone called them, achieved celebrity status almost immediately. The group flocked around them to hear their stories, and everyone wanted to volunteer on their daily supply runs.

They were leading people further away than was necessary in Lexi's opinion, and an awkward moment ensued when one of them – she couldn't tell them apart – asked to use her Discovery so that they could be more comfortable. The look of pure loathing she gave them only prompted laughter, which didn't improve her opinion of them.

She still didn't trust them, nor did she like their over-familiar attitudes towards people. She found herself wondering what Penny would have made of them; *mincemeat*, was the likely answer. Two impertinent, loud and rude young men would not have been tolerated by the stern woman, and Lexi could almost imagine their faces as she sat them down to be reprimanded.

Only Penny wouldn't be able to do that.

Penny was dead, Dan was gone, Steve was in a coma and Lexi was losing control of the group. The Rangers had been crippled after the group split, and when Steve crashed the helicopter, she had been left completely on her own. Now, the gullible council had been sucked into the bullshit the two newcomers were spouting. They were lapping it up, and had power, authority, guns and the run of the whole place.

She asked Rich his opinion about them, but he was tight-lipped and barely answered other than to nod in agreement or shake his head. She pretended not to notice that he had been drinking sometimes, as much as it worried her, but to turn on one of the few who would still support her didn't seem like a sensible play. She knew the ship was sinking, and she had to decide whether to be a rat or not.

EYE IN THE SKY

Mitch was happy. Mitch was usually amused by everything and rarely felt upset or annoyed, but despite his years as a professional soldier, he actually felt excited about what they were doing right then.

He was in the crow's nest on the boat, looking down on the small compound being temporarily fortified. What he really wanted to see was a herd of deer strolling past, and he scanned the countryside repeatedly hoping for such a sight. This constant search for food served to keep him alert in all directions.

He had the big battle rifle beside him, but that would be heard for miles around on a still day like it was. Instead, he used his suppressed carbine similar to Dan's to methodically search the ground. He never thought of himself as such, but Mitch was a man of very small comforts who needed little to keep him going.

That was one of the reasons for his happiness: he was well equipped, he had food and water, and he had a purpose. He was comfortable enough, but having never spent every evening sitting in the comfort of his own home on his own sofa meant the experience was relative, he supposed. He watched as Dan started up a motorbike with Neil doing the same alongside him. Mitch saw that they only had their basic personal equipment with them, and guessed it was purely a short reconnaissance mission; anything they saw which they wanted could be collected with a plan that way.

The rolling gate which formed part of the fence squealed horribly like a tortured metal animal as the two men on bikes were waved off, only for the agonising sound to reach his ears again as the gate was secured.

So offended was Mitch by the noise that he reached for the small radio beside the big rifle. "Adam, it's Mitch," he said curtly, repeating it twice out of habit.

"Yo!" came the response a second later. Mitch buried his instinctive non-commissioned officer's reaction to poor radio discipline and gently reminded himself that there was no British Army any longer and this kid wasn't really a soldier. He took a breath and answered him without overreacting.

"Grab a couple more pairs of hands and search the buildings for any kind of oil, will you?" he said.

"Oil?" came the bewildered response as Adam stopped and turned to face the direction of the crow's nest.

Mitch could see him clearly because of the zoom on his optic, but he was fairly certain Adam wouldn't be able to make out anything other than a small shape.

"Yes," he replied, allowing some annoyance to creep into his voice as though he were talking to a child who was being intentionally obtuse. "Some oil. Any kind of oil really, as long as it stops those gates from waking the dead next time they open. Understood?" he finished sarcastically.

Adam understood. Sketching a salute in Mitch's general direction, he turned to do as he had been told.

Now that small interruption was over, Mitch turned back to look for any sign of fresh meat as the group below busied themselves making their little corner of the world more comfortable. Wooden pallets were being carried into the building, no doubt to fashion some kind of furniture. A few people had been equipped by Jack, who was still busy cooking the enormous seafood barbecue medley, and sent with the discarded pieces of fish to use as bait for yet more fresh produce. Mitch could see Henry, Pip, Jimmy and Sera talking happily as they dangled their legs off the jetty while they fished.

He saw Emma pacing by herself at the side of the building, talking with her hands as she explained something to the small digital recorder she always carried with her. He liked that about her; it was her thing to always be keeping some kind of record of what they were doing.

What, or more specifically who, he couldn't see caused him some concern. The kid was tough and he liked her a lot. For him to trust teenagers who had been trained by the Army was difficult enough for him, but he never questioned her ability or dedication after he had seen her work. He thought it was human nature, although the clever people would probably have a name for a syndrome or something. He saw it simply that she was a natural survivor and a fast learner; when coupled with a strong mentor and good instruction then she excelled. She was, in his opinion, a fantastic little killer.

Only she was pretty badly banged up right now, and having never seen her cry or act like a kid, he doubted it was anything short of serious. In fact, he was sure that the same knock to the head would have put himself or Dan out of action.

A man of very private faith, he uttered a short prayer under his breath for her speedy recovery and hoped that the great lump of a dog was keeping watch over her. As well as Kate, obviously.

A glance over the scope told him that there were probably four hours of daylight left, and as per the standard operating procedures he had followed with unwavering indoctrination for many years, he would remain at his post until after the sun was fully down.

That gave him a few hours to find something for them to eat.

BORN TO BE WILD

Dan didn't feel at all like a wild biker, but Neil had sung the song out loud for the first mile of their trip inland – at least the words he knew of it – and even over the sound of their bikes, Dan couldn't get the damned tune out of his head.

Despite Neil's levity, they travelled cautiously, being mindful not to stumble blindly into anyone's territory and invite a negative reaction. Dan supposed that was what the world had reverted to now: territory. Each group, formed out of a deep instinctive understanding that numbers equalled safety, had laid claim to their own small patch of the world just as they had done, and would defend their people and their resources against anyone else.

Humans, at least in most parts of the world, he guessed, had become both predator and prey.

Cruising along smooth, open roads, they passed industrial areas interspersed with open fields. Each building they approached prompted them to slow and assess it for signs of human activity and to check if they could see anything on their shopping list.

Dan ran through that list again in his head. It was simple: vehicles, fuel, food and water. All things that would have been very easy to come by before and immediately after the world changed, but now nature had begun the slow offensive to take back everything created by man, the availability of resources was dwindling.

The horizon ahead of them was dominated by the higher buildings of a more built-up area that, despite his normal rules of avoidance, Dan was heading straight for. He wanted to be equipped, stocked and on the road inside of three days.

As they approached the outskirts, a few abandoned vehicles presented an opportunity to start ticking off the list. A large van for transporting their equipment would be ideal, and more than a few were present. On closer inspection, all of them had perished tyres and one had been transformed into a surreal greenhouse as the open window had let in the elements and now the seats had become a bed of weeds. They gave up on checking anything left out in the open, and the odds of finding vehicles which had been left under cover greatly reduced their chances of quick success.

A brief conversation about these diminished odds made them turn away from the town and return to the industrial areas instead. After three hours and a significant amount of energy expended in breaking in, they found a suitable vehicle to start their temporary fleet. High-sided and with a long wheelbase, a white Mercedes Sprinter stood proudly in one of the units, largely untouched by the brief passage of time which had destroyed so many like it left to the mercy of the weather. Predictably, the battery was dead, and the two men hunted around the unit for anything to get it started with. They were out of luck and would have to return with a mobile charger pack. The unit had vending machines that had been ruthlessly pillaged for their contents. At the very least, they would need another vehicle like this to have enough room to move their people and the gear they had brought, and even then it would be in little or no comfort.

Dan felt suddenly very foreign; all the posters and signs around him were predominantly in French, and his basic understanding of the language left him mostly guessing. Even the van being left-hand drive was strange. It hit him again just how far they were away from home, or at least the home they had built and left.

They began to work their way back towards their boatyard, checking the other buildings along the way. By the time they had made it back, the sun was already sinking. The metal gates were rolled back by Adam, neither of the returning men noticing that they slid along almost soundlessly in comparison with their earlier departure.

Jack was in the same spot by his crafted barbeque, seemingly not having moved earlier in the day, only this time instead of fish, the smell of roasting meat floated to Dan's nostrils.

His raised brow was met by Marie's smile and an explanation that Mitch had shot two rabbits and a deer while they had been gone. The prospect of fresh meat had gathered a small crowd as they relished the smell in the air. Dan turned to face the crow's nest and sketched a small salute to the soldier he couldn't see, thanking him for the provisions. He asked Adam to take over from Mitch until sundown, and the eager young man jogged away, only too happy to comply. He had taken to his new role easily, and Dan wondered why he had never asked to become a Ranger before. He was comfortable doing the job he had been given, he imagined. Only the prospect of new adventures had prompted his willingness to be trained in the more violent skills possessed by members of the group. The heavy burden of his choices and responsibilities made Dan question some things, such as would Adam have been caught unawares like Joe was? Could Joe still be alive if he had recognised Adam's abilities?

Shaking away the what ifs, he turned to see a welcome sight.

Leah was up and on her feet, walking slowly towards him. She looked smaller and younger without the ballistic vest, although he saw she still wore a Walther on her hip and was no doubt carrying a couple of knives somewhere. He beamed at her improved state and asked her how she felt.

"Still a big groggy," she replied, sipping from a cup before offering him some. "Headache from hell, but I can move my neck more now, which is nice."

"Well, I'm glad you're feeling better," he replied genuinely. "When will Kate let you back out to play?" he asked, worried that he was pushing her too hard again.

"Tomorrow," she answered with a smile. "She said 'we'll see,' but it'll be tomorrow."

As the sun dropped, the whole group assembled for their portion of meat to supplement the canned food. As they ate, Dan reported on their scouting.

"We've found one big van and one smaller one. Both will need some work to get them going, and we'll need something else with more seats if we want to travel in comfort, but we should get on our way as soon as possible." Nods from the faces watching him made him continue. "We need to siphon off the remaining fuel from the boat and take the starter packs to get the vans back. That's tomorrow's plans, and I need Neil, Jimmy and Leah to come with me first thing. Mitch will stay here in the nest to keep watch, and everyone else carry on getting the kit organised."

As usual, they melted away to their own corners and conversations for the evening.

HOSTILE TERRITORY

The morning went as planned, and Mitch watched the two motor-bikes carry the four bodies away from the compound. Adam wheeled back the metal gates and threw a small wave in his direction before he went to get some sleep after keeping watch during the night.

Mitch settled in for another motionless day in the heat, having added a tarpaulin to the nest to fend off the worst of the sun.

Leah held tight to Dan as they weaved their ungainly way towards their first objective. The two cleared the building in their familiar, intrinsic way, as each knew the other's thoughts and barely needed to communicate. The smaller van was started after a while and it coughed into life as it barked out a black cloud of unburnt fuel. It was left running as renewed life pulsed around the engine, like it had been brought back from the brink of death by a kind of mechanical resuscitation.

Jimmy drove it back to base escorted by Neil, leaving the other two to continue on to the second prize. Again, the routine of clearing the building served to sharpen Leah's skills, as she had been laid up for a few days. The bigger van started more easily, and the teenager climbed behind the wheel.

"Never driven a left-hand drive," she said to Dan.

"You're only little," he answered. "You shouldn't have driven anything yet!"

She thought about that, then nodded to herself. "Good point," she accepted.

They followed the return route expecting to be back by midday, when everything changed.

Mitch heard Jimmy's return long before he drove into sight. He brought the van into the compound and turned it to park by their adopted building where it could be easily loaded. Mitch returned to his methodical scanning of the countryside, settling back into his rhythm as he half-listened to the conversations heard from below him.

A flash of movement caught his eye, making him instinctively twitch the scope back to it.

His first thought was that it must be Dan and Leah coming back.

His second thought, immediately afterwards, was that it was coming from the wrong direction.

Adrenaline surged through his body like high-octane fuel dumped straight into an idling engine. Switching to the big rifle, he called a loud and authoritative warning down to the others.

"Get inside!" he bawled. "Incoming vehicles!"

Stunned silence followed his shout as the group stared in his direction before common sense and self-preservation startled them into action. Like rats in the dark bathed in sudden light, they scattered in panic, leaving only Jimmy, Neil and Adam scrambling into cover.

He snatched up the small radio next to him and tried to raise Dan. Twice he called into the mic with his ingrained calm and succinct speech. Twice he received no answer. For now, they were on their own.

He watched as the movement became a convoy of three vehicles heading directly towards them, sun glinting from windscreens. As they neared and the heat haze dissipated, Mitch could make out that the lead car was marked like a police vehicle. He racked his brains to try and remember anything about the Belgian police and came up with nothing other than that they had local and national forces like much of Europe. Not that jurisdictional matters held sway anymore, but it was his soldier's instincts to try and know as much as he could about any potential enemy. Knowledge was power, but a height advantage and a big rifle always helped.

Painstakingly, the convoy made its slow approach and split up as they neared. One vehicle remained at a distance, the other looped off-road to the open ground on his left and the last made straight for the gates.

He switched his aim between the two closest cars, waiting for signs of hostility. He grabbed for the radio again and called Marie. She answered from the building below him over the sounds of anxious chatter in the room.

"Keep trying to get hold of Dan," he told her, "and keep every-one inside."

She acknowledged him, and proceeded to call Dan and Leah in a calm voice, clear and precise.

The vehicle parked facing the gates was clearly visible in his sights now. The words *Police Fédérale* were emblazoned across the front in white lettering over the dust-covered drab blue paint. The passenger door opened and from inside came a man wearing the black and blue of a police uniform. He wore a heavy vest not unlike their own, and Mitch's trained eye recognised the automatic Steyr rifle he carried. He hefted the ugly gun with no malice, but the threat was still very evident.

Eight miles away, the radio crackled uselessly in a pouch on Dan's vest, drowned out by the noise of the motorbike he rode following Leah driving the van.

The man dressed vaguely as a Belgian federal police officer strolled towards the gates, unconcerned. Confident. Arrogant, almost. His uniform showed signs of wear, and Mitch doubted that the wild beard would have been within the uniform standards when his state of dress still mattered. He stopped well short of the perimeter and called out in French. He didn't hear the words, not that he could have understood them if he had, but the voice was harsh and guttural. Watching him through the scope, Mitch wondered if others saw them with the same fear as he saw these men now.

Adam shouted something back from behind his barricade of barrels and wooden pallets, probably to tell the man he didn't understand him. It frustrated Mitch that he couldn't hear the words; it left vital information out of his assessment. He could do little from where he was unless the shooting started, and then he could pour fire at them mercilessly with his height advantage and commanding position; the heavy rounds from the big rifle could cut through the skin of the cars with horrific ease. He scanned to the other vehicles – no movement.

He put himself in the position of the intruders. What would he do if he was planning to storm the compound? He wouldn't walk up to the gates in broad daylight for starters, and if he had, then he would have sent others to flank their position. He stayed calm, assessed the facts, and hoped his conclusion that they weren't hostile was correct.

He had to wait until he was in play, and every second ticked by in slow torment.

Adam had cowered behind the barricades they had built and glanced over at Jimmy, who wore a look of terror. Adam thought he probably wore the same look. A glance over the makeshift wall showed a big man in uniform walking towards them holding a rifle he had never seen before. He ducked back down and waited for the shooting to start. He completely embarrassed himself when the man shouted to them.

"We don't speak Belgian," he called back.

A gruff laugh sounded in response. "What about French? There is no Belgian language! Who are you, and where did you come from?" the intruder growled back.

Adam looked over the barricade again. The man was smiling, just not that kindly.

"We're from England," Adam shouted in simple explanation.

Another laugh returned, as though the explanation of their origins suddenly made sense of their ignorance. "That explains your trespass," he said, stumbling over finding the right word. "This area is controlled by my unit. We have established," another pause as his brain searched for the correct vocabulary, "borders. This is our area and you are not here with our permission."

Adam was about to answer when the man continued.

"But no matter! You did not know, so this is OK. Now, who is your leader? Send them out to speak to me and we can make arrangements."

Adam didn't want to say that their leader was out stealing vehicles from this man's territory. His silence as he thought did not impress the man.

"I am Commissaire Divisionnaire Alexandre Renard. I formally order you to surrender your commander to me so that we may come to terms. You have ten minutes."

With that, he turned and strode purposefully away from the gates.

Leah's sharp eyes nearly cost Dan his life. The alien shape on the horizon morphed into a vehicle from a distance far enough for their approach not to have been noticed with any luck. Her sudden braking nearly took Dan off the motorbike, forcing him to swerve desperately to avoid ploughing into the back of the van.

His terror was short-lived. By the time he had stopped the bike and turned to demand an explanation, he saw she was out of the van and gazing intently through the scope of her carbine. Whatever he was going to say to her evaporated instantly as he swung up his own gun to see what she was looking at.

A van, parked facing the gates of their compound. Dan scrabbled at the Velcro of his pouch to free the radio.

"Mitch, it's Dan," he said in a low, disciplined tone.

"Here. Can you see them?" came the instant response.

"Yes. What's going on?"

"Not sure, can't hear them from up here. Two other vehicles; one in the distance, one to the south just sitting tight. One just came to the gate carrying a Steyr."

Dan absorbed this information quickly. His group were loosely surrounded by an armed and organised enemy – at least, he assumed they were an enemy. As he was digesting it, another voice came over the radio.

"Dan, it's Marie." She sounded stressed, but was clearly forcing her words to come over the radio as controlled.

"Here. Go on," he answered.

"Their leader is some kind of policeman and he's given us ten minutes to give him our leader to talk. Says we're on their territory."

"OK," Dan replied, closing his eyes briefly to think. "Everyone sit tight. I'll go and talk to him. Marie, keep everyone else inside out of sight, and Mitch, stay sharp in case it goes noisy. Understood?"

"Yes," said Marie.

"Roger," came Mitch's voice.

His mind racing, he turned to Leah to ask her to do something dangerous. Again.

Calling the girl to him, he explained what he needed. She absorbed it blankly, seemingly without emotion, until she envisioned how he hoped it would play out. A slow smile spread across her cheeks as she understood her part in the show.

TEMPORARY REPRIEVE

Lizzie was ripped from her uncomfortable sleep by a shout from Alice. Recently, she had been so exhausted that sleep came instantly whenever she closed her eyes, but it was a restless sleep that was only ever a blink from consciousness.

She was instantly awake, flying from the chair she occupied and finding herself staring down at Steve's eyes.

Which were open.

He stared at them blankly, taking long and slow blinks to clear his senses as the fog of his battered brain tried desperately to make sense of what had happened and where he was. Lizzie snatched the tiny light in the top pocket of her scrubs and checked his pupils, making him wince at the harsh light and close his eyes again.

A rasping groan escaped his dry throat. Alice gave him water with a straw and saw the evident pain and pleasure he took simultaneously from the cool liquid running down into his stomach. His mouth and lips moved with seemingly great effort as he tried to speak. Both women bent down to him to hear what he had to say.

Agonising seconds passed as he tried to get the words out, until finally a hoarse whisper sounded faintly.

"How long," he managed to ask before a racking cough forced his eyes to close tightly with the torment his body went through.

Lizzie snatched up keys to a locked cabinet and quickly prepared a syringe of morphine. Only she and Kate knew of its presence, and it was a secret entrusted to her when she became Head of Medical. She carefully applied it to the drip in his arm and gave the bag a gentle squeeze to flush the drug into his system with a small push of the saline solution behind it. Instantly, Steve's eyes grew a little wider and his tense body relaxed as the pain ebbed away.

She didn't want to give him much, just enough that he wouldn't be in agony. There wasn't much of a supply to keep him going for long, but she didn't doubt his ability to take some pain. His pupils shrunk slightly, and a sigh of almost satisfaction escaped his mouth.

Too much, as he lapsed again into unconsciousness. Only this time it was sleep, not coma.

"Go tell your dad," Lizzie instructed Alice.

As the girl skipped away, Lizzie carefully locked away the morphine and returned to her chair, dozing off instantly into a deeper sleep than she had experienced in over a week.

NEGOTIATIONS

Commissaire Divisionnaire Alexandre Renard was not a patient man.

He was not a man to suffer fools, either. A former paratrooper in the Belgian armed forces, his ruthless efficiency and borderline brutality had made his ascent through the ranks of the federal police swift and notable. After the collapse of society, he had enlisted every survivor he found and pressed them all into a daily regimen of physical activity and strict order.

They had established a defensible home, farming, trade, supply routes and eventually agreed borders with other factions to prevent conflict over resources. Some groups he had encountered did not agree with his terms, and their numbers had mostly added to his own group. He was not a cruel man, but his leadership style was undeniably harsher than Dan's.

His scouts had reported activity at the boatyard to their superiors, and those reports had landed on his desk the day before. Now he had found these trespassers to be Englishmen cowering behind boxes, he felt less threatened by their presence.

But the trespass could not go unanswered, or his own forces would lose respect for him. He maintained order by such rules, and he liked order. The invaders would have to leave, but they would not take any resources from his territory.

Shortly after he had delivered his demands to speak to their leader and returned to his vehicle, an engine note pierced the air. He gazed north to see a white van driving slowly in his direction.

He turned to the two other men in his car and spoke to them in French, pointing out that the English had already stolen a vehicle. Mirthless laughter answered him, as the other two men thought their commander was making a joke. He wasn't, and his scowl let them know that they had read him wrong.

The van pulled up about fifty metres from him, and he stood stock-still in the road, feet braced, waiting to meet the driver.

Renard saw a man climb down from behind the wheel. Dressed in black, armed, and carrying himself like he knew his trade. At last, someone professional that he could relate to and not a conscript. As the man approached, Renard saw that he was almost half a head shorter than himself and looked tough, although this man bore an evil scar down the left side of his face which he imagined lesser men would fear.

He stopped ten paces away and stood, saying nothing.

Renard introduced himself, investing fierce pride in his rank and status, adding that he was the commander of a large force in control of this territory. He addressed him in accented English, assuming the man did not speak French.

He assumed correctly, and Dan annoyed him by responding only with his first name. Renard sighed and made a show of slowly slinging his gun on his back. Dan responded to the gesture in kind, mutually agreeing to talk without the fear of violence. Yet.

"Cut to the chase," Dan said. "What's the problem?"

"The problem?" scoffed Renard. "The problem, my English friend, is that you are all trespassing and have taken resources from my territory. You must leave, and you will not be permitted to take this vehicle with you. How did you get here?"

"By sea, obviously," Dan said in his calm, mocking tone he used when talking to someone with a superiority complex. He looked away and took his time lighting a cigarette, before grudgingly offering one to the leader of the opposition. Renard ignored his gesture.

"Specifically," Renard said, carefully enunciating each syllable.

"A yacht. It's moored in there," he said, pointing without looking to his left.

Renard's eyebrows twitched slightly, indicating maybe some hidden lust for opulence.

"How can we get through this without any unpleasantness?" Dan asked the Belgian.

"We can do one of two things," he said. "We can walk in and take what you have for trespassing and you can join us, or you can leave with nothing."

So the horse trade started with a lame nag, thought Dan.

"There are other options, and I doubt you'll find either of your solutions easy to achieve," Dan replied coolly.

Renard scoffed again. "Really? How so? You have a few people with guns and I have all of my people with guns. I do not bring civilians on missions. Please, tell me your options." He laughed at him.

"Well, we could appeal to your sense of morality to let us go unharmed, we could trade, or we could all shoot each other and see who's left afterwards. I'm in a bit of a hurry to get off your *territory* and I'd rather save my ammunition, if that helps you come to any decision."

Renard laughed again. "Tell me how the few of you can fight all of us?"

Dan didn't respond to the taunts born of nervousness and arrogance. He simply and quietly laid out a few facts.

"Because I've got a sniper with a high-powered rifle looking directly at you, and he can take out your people in the car to the south. He's a remarkably good shot, so he can probably put another ten shots into your backup vehicle afterwards. Other than that, you'll find that all of my people are armed, and storming in there would be bad for your long-term health. I've got other things, but I'll leave those where they are for now."

He saw Renard bridle at the calm counter-threats and instantly his trained eye fixed onto the highest point.

"So you have a sniper up the mast of that boat and a few guns. Can your sniper see in the dark, I wonder?"

Dan bit back the retort that he couldn't, but he could still shoot very accurately in very poor light. No point in showing all your cards.

Renard continued his verbal chess-like assault, trying to outplay, out-think and out-boast Dan's claims.

"I can have a hundred armed men here by tonight. I doubt you even have that many bullets."

That was inaccurate, but what they did have had to last, and they couldn't afford to waste ammo, let alone any lives in getting out of this situation.

"Look," Dan reasoned, "we're a lot like you. We formed a big group and defended our territory, but I assure you we just need a couple of vehicles to get on our way. We have places to be and we're on a timeframe, so please, what's it going to take?"

"You do not have anything to trade us in return for your safe passage?" he enquired politely.

"You can have our boat. I'm assured it was worth millions before."

"What if we take the boat anyway?"

"Then most of our people on both sides of this fence would die because we can't come to an agreement. We are at the start of quite a long journey, and we would appreciate it if you let us go on our way." He tried the emotional sell to seal the deal. "My woman is pregnant, and I'm sure you know what that means for her."

He saw Renard's face fall slightly.

"Yes, I do," he replied. "Are you telling me there is something that can be done?"

It was Dan's turn to look crestfallen.

"We don't know, not for sure, but have you figured out why we survived yet?"

The look on Renard's face said that he hadn't, although he probably didn't have his own virologist PhD student hiding a hundred yards away.

"Africa. You've been to Africa, right?"

Renard looked like he had been slapped. "Yes. Is that the reason we did not die?" he asked, open-mouthed.

Dan had guessed his regime didn't include much in the way of research. "Like I said, we don't know, but that's where we're going to try and find out."

Renard made a show of thinking, even though Dan suspected he would still attempt to extract some form of payment. Dan had kept him talking long enough for his risky backup plan to be ready, although he could see no sign of it, and decided to end negotiations.

Dan took a deep breath as though weary, held it, then let it out in a low whistle. As Renard eyed him suspiciously, a noise sounded behind him.

Leah had crept low and as fast as stealth would allow along the deep drainage ditch at the side of the road. Luckily, it had been a hot summer, and it was mostly dry save for a few boggy parts which her nimble feet avoided easily. Her small stature made approaching invisibly in full daylight relatively easy, and she was close enough to hear the conversation when her signal came.

Silently, she sprang from the ditch and approached their van from behind. The rear passenger was out of the vehicle and stood watching the two men talk, concentrating on the foreign language and woefully unaware of his surroundings.

Leaving the carbine slung on her back, she decided that a show of force would be more effective; there were too many targets in a small space to use the carbine properly anyway.

Creeping behind the standing man, she saw another in the driver's seat with the door open. Neither were even the slightest bit concerned with the direction she had come from, and both stared intently at the conversation, which, to her, closely resembled two grumpy peacocks displaying their tail feathers.

She drew the Walther from behind her right hip and with her left hand, she unsheathed the blade she wore high on her chest. She straightened up, took two long strides forward to gather momentum and delivered a hard kick to the back of the standing man's right knee. He dropped instantly to his knees, but the sudden appearance of a wickedly sharp blade at his throat stopped him from pitching forwards any further. He froze with a strangled cry to accompany the yelp brought on by his pained joint.

At this sound, the driver spun to look only to find himself staring into the barrel of her gun pointed straight at his head. Both neutralised, both completely at her mercy. If her man on the floor made a move, he would die with a severed carotid artery, and the other man was too close to run but too far away to try and rush her before she shot him.

"Checkmate," she said aloud.

"One of the other things I mentioned," Dan said casually. "Not a threat, merely a demonstration that we are more than capable of defending ourselves. But we are good people, and we don't want bloodshed."

"And my men?" asked Renard angrily, annoyed more at himself for the incompetence of his men. "What am I to tell the others when I let you go?"

"Tell them you let us go in exchange for the boat. Tell them we have women and children. Tell them we're idiots who you don't want hanging around here. We're mostly English, so they should believe that. Say whatever you have to say to save face, but we are leaving."

With that, Dan gave another short, low whistle and saw from the corner of his eye how Leah withdrew the knife so fast the man checked with his hand to see if she had slashed him. She backed away a distance before lowering the gun and returning to Dan's side.

Renard seemed speechless at what had just happened. He was shocked and told Dan as much.

"Where did you get her?" he asked in awe.

"Secret KGB training programme for child assassins. Got her off the internet." With that, he turned and walked away. "We'll be gone by morning, and I do hope you keep your word," Dan shouted back as he reached the van.

CUT SHORT

The sight of Dan rolling back in with the vehicle they needed and showing no concern made some of the group feel foolish. They weren't, he told them; they had all done exactly what they should have done. He grabbed up the radio to ask Mitch to sit tight and report their next move before gathering everyone inside.

"We're leaving," he announced. "I said we were going in the morning, but we will be going sooner than that. Everybody load up their kit and find space in a van – I know it's not comfortable, but needs must. Everyone go, pack up."

The packing began immediately. He caught the eyes of Marie and Neil, nodding them over to him. They found a quiet corner and brought Mitch in via radio.

He quickly recited his conversation with Renard, leaving out the most brutal of Leah's actions in tipping the power balance.

"Basically they're like us, but also not at the same time. It's certainly no Slaver's Bay, but they run things differently, and it looks like we've unwittingly walked into claimed territory. We're leaving with what we have and technically trading them the boat for it. That's the face value of it anyway. Real answer is that if he brought his entire force, then his losses would be huge and so would ours. Neither of us can cope with that. He was just about to call my bluff, I think, when Leah appeared having taken down two of his guards inside of a couple of seconds."

"Yay me!" said Leah in quiet sarcasm.

Mitch's amusement was plain in the laughter they heard over the radio before his voice returned to the professional soldier he was.

"They're withdrawing now. Doubt they'll go far."

Dan asked him to stay on it. Mitch assured him that he would, but asked for Adam to pick his kit up for him.

Dan walked outside, lit a cigarette and wondered if the coffee had been tipped away yet. Leah walked to his side carrying her kit, a crooked smile cracking on her face.

"I said sneak up and show yourself, not show off," he reproved her gently.

She shrugged in response, the smile growing wider.

"You'll get old like me one day," he said, goading her, "then a concussion will put you out for longer."

She turned as she walked away, effortlessly pacing backwards without a change of pace to stick her tongue out at him.

The vans were being packed as efficiently as they could be in a hurry, but people would still be cramped in on top of bags and boxes. To save space, Mitch, Dan and Neil would ride the bikes. Jack would drive the big van and Jimmy the smaller one. Seeing how much stuff they were cramming into the vehicles, Dan thought that riding a motorcycle through the cold night would be better than playing sardines.

Leah was asked to ride shotgun with Jack, Adam with Jimmy. Putting Ash in the back of a van with no windows and people to bite would not have been a good idea, so he rode up front with Marie and Leah, excited about the commotion.

Dan called Mitch down from the nest, shuddering as he watched him make the reverse climb. He took the big rifle from him and double-checked that he would be fit to ride, receiving the answer he knew he would. Mitch was fine. You could ask Mitch to rob a beehive wearing nothing but a smile and flowers in his hair and he'd still say it was fine.

He passed over the large rifle to Leah, who rested it on the dash of their van. They had the map out and were pointing out the quickest way from the area.

"Through this tunnel here, straight through to the city," said Marie.

Dan opened his mouth to speak but heard his own words in a higher and sweeter voice before he could say them out loud.

"No. Perfect ambush point. The most direct route will be the best place to get caught. We need to head east then south to avoid the city and the tunnels."

She looked between Dan and Marie, waiting to see whose side he would take.

"No tunnels. Take point and navigate us." With that, Dan turned away to dig out a windcheater from his pack before slinging it in the back of the big van. His thin tactical gloves would have to suffice, but he knew he was in for an uncomfortable night.

Searching the busy faces for his old Irishman, he found him and told him exactly what he wanted from him. As the understanding washed over him, a cruel smile spread slowly from his mouth to the deep lines of his crinkled brow.

They had managed to siphon a dozen jerrycans of fuel from the boat, which should get them a good distance into Germany. He hoped.

The bikes were topped off from the cans with the red stripes, and they were good to go. People piled in to settle in whatever soft part they could find, happy to be leaving behind the chance of more hostilities.

Dan fired up his motorcycle and scanned around. They were good to go. He slapped on the side of the big van twice to signal their departure and took one last look towards the harbour.

In the dying light, he could still make out the name on the stern of the boat as it rose and fell gently in the water. He had to assure himself that they were just leaving a boat behind, but riding away from *Hope* seemed a little too poignant at that moment.

NINE LIVES

The gathered crowd were kept at bay outside the door to medical and only a select few were permitted access to Steve. He was in a great deal of discomfort and could only speak for a few minutes at a time before pain overcame his senses again.

As the story of what had happened during and since the crash was absorbed by him, he asked for Chris to visit so he could thank him for getting him out. Chris's tears of anger were misunderstood by many, but Steve knew who he blamed for recent events. Truth be told, Steve harboured more than a little resentment for Dan and the others who left, as it was becoming apparent just how fragile their small corner of the world had become.

Lexi desperately wanted to pour out the events since he crash-landed back home, but even she could see just how weak he was. It would have to wait until he could absorb the information and hopefully back up her suspicions about the twins.

Now that he was having periods of lucidity, Lizzie could examine him more thoroughly. Other than a few broken ribs – nothing could really be done for them – and the mess of his leg, it seemed that the whole of his body had taken a severe beating; it was as though he'd gone through an industrial dryer with a dozen house bricks on high spin.

After the others had been banished to allow him to rest, Alice sat with him and fed him mouthfuls of soup. One sentence at a time, he told her how he had now survived three helicopter crashes.

A hint of a smile broke the lines in his cheeks as he told the girl about the others, both in training, and how his commander when he retired called him a cat with nine lives.

"I reckon I've used up eight by now," he said quietly, "so I think I need to take it easy."

Lexi was speaking to Paul in Ops when Rich walked in. He seemed surprised to see anyone else there and began to mutter apologies.

"Don't be silly," she said to him, "there's few enough of us left as it is."

She went to pour him a drink out of habit, then remembered herself and switched aim to put an unnecessary top-up into her own glass. She knew he had been drinking but convinced herself that it would work itself out. In truth, she couldn't face having to deal with it when everything was up in the air.

As they sat discussing Steve's return from the dead, the two new-comers walked in. The twins' conversation stopped instantly when they saw they weren't alone. They ignored them with utter disdain and turned away to the armoury. Without a word, they helped themselves to automatic weapons, took the keys to a Defender and left without another word.

"Those two are up to something," said Paul, voicing the obvious suspicions of all three of them.

"But it's only us who see it," finished Lexi.

"They operate outside of our standard practices. They have the ear of certain people and they are popular. We can't compete with that, not with things as they are right now," said Rich quietly, surprising the other two. He had just said more words in one sentence than he had to anyone in a month.

"So what do we do about them?" asked Paul.

"Follow them," said Rich, standing up from his chair with more purpose than he had felt since the raid on the Welsh invaders. He saw this as a chance to make up for his lapse, to prove his worth once again, to turn his back on the depression he had allowed himself to spiral into.

Paul and Lexi rose with him, but Rich stopped them.

"No. This is on me." He took a sidearm, loaded two magazines and picked up keys before leaving without another word.

The sound of a second engine pulling away from the house faded into the distance as Lexi and Paul sat in silence. Paul reached over and refreshed their drinks, leaving the empty air heavy with words unsaid.

UNCOMFORTABLE MEMORIES

Dan carefully nursed his motorcycle along the roads flanking the two laden vans as they travelled south then east out of Belgium; the seat had made him numb and the cool night air was slowly freezing every exposed patch of skin. He ached throughout his entire body, but he couldn't risk the lives of everyone just because he wanted a rest.

It felt alien, dangerous even, to be driving through the night with lights on. Anyone within ten miles of them would be alerted to their vulnerable presence.

Not since they had fled their temporary camp at the supermarket so many months ago had they journeyed at night with lights, and the feelings of that terrified flight brought back the same fearful sense of desperation he had experienced then, of bringing a group of frightened people away from safety and into an uncertain future. Last time it had worked out; this time he hoped his luck would remain.

As dawn broke, they crossed two consecutive bridges and passed into Germany. There was no sense of ceremony. No celebration. Just exhausted progress, another milestone in their journey.

The four-way flashers on the van illuminated for the third time during the night, signifying the need to stop for a comfort break. Dan sent up a silent prayer of thanks and responded by twisting the throttle and gunning his motorcycle ahead of their small convoy to search for a safe place to sit tight for the day. Mitch followed, tireless as ever, and the rest of the convoy hung back while they cleared a small fuel station.

The vehicles were hidden away from the road and the group trooped into the building in silence. Cramped muscles and lack of sleep had stifled all conversation, and even prevented the ritual of hot drinks. People shuffled in, found themselves a comfortable corner and crashed.

Dan sat, closing his eyes for just a minute. He woke to his shoulder being shaken by Adam, offering to take the night shift. He could only nod his thanks as his body failed him. Marie sat next to him, wordlessly unclipping his carbine from the sling attached to his vest and laying him down despite his weak protestations. He fought internally with himself to stay awake, to be alert and protect his group. He had to accept, to trust, to allow others to take the burden he always tried to take on himself. He had barely slept more than a few hours in one go since before they left home.

Home. His thoughts drifted away with his consciousness, thinking that he had lost the right to call it home now. He had found it, cleared it, made it their home and now he had abandoned it. Abandoned the others who trusted him.

Tormented, tired, he fell soundly asleep with a tortured conscience.

TOO LITTLE, TOO LATE

Renard was unhappy at being out-played, to put it mildly. He was extremely unhappy with his two companions and let them know his opinion about them being bested by a child at length and with much use of threats and foul language.

He promised not to punish their incompetence in return for their total support of his version of events. That version detailed how he was a merciful and magnanimous leader, and that he had promised to allow them to leave because he pitied their plight.

He then assembled a force of fifty fighting men and women, put his best-trained at the front, and prepared for an attack under cover of darkness.

As they crept forward in the cool night air, he located the sentry he had left on the southern road. He reported no movement, meaning that the ill-trained fools had believed they could safely leave in the daylight and not face any penalty for embarrassing him.

As the group split off into three prongs to attack the compound, he relished the moment when he would take the suppressed weapon from the man who refused to accord him the proper respect. Maybe he could be put to work on one of the farming parties? He was sure he wouldn't let him be armed; there was an edge to the man he would never trust. A fire still burned not far from the entrance, bathing the area in a warm, red glow.

When the three prongs of the attack were in position, he sent up the signal, prompting the first wave to attack.

The gates, curiously unlocked and unguarded, were thrown open with next to no noise. A war cry went up as his troops stormed the compound and kicked open the doors of the buildings.

The cheers died away when they found nobody inside.

Striding through the gaggle of his uncertain militia, he made straight for the yacht, the technical prize of his assault.

As he walked purposefully down the wooden gangplank, a slight resistance tugged at the ankle of his trousers, making him stop and turn. A popping sound behind him echoed ominously. A wave of heat and an invisible pressure wave pushed against him. His eyes widened in disbelief, then terror, as he dived headlong into the black water below.

~

The thin wire Jack had painstakingly strung between two posts had worked perfectly. As Renard walked through it, the far end of his trap had pulled the trigger of the flare gun and launched the bright missile into the main cabin where almost all of the remaining petrol had been intentionally spilt. The flare caught the fumes even before the projectile had struck home, and the confined space only amplified the ignition.

It didn't explode – it would have had to be pressurised for that to happen, he had explained to Dan earlier – but it did go up fast.

The flames erupted from the cabin, blowing out the small round windows with the force of the fire desperately seeking a better supply of oxygen. By the time Renard had surfaced and looked back, the boat was engulfed in flames.

He had been beaten again and was now deprived of any spoils. Angrily climbing the rocks to reach dry land, he raged at the assembled men and women as he demanded to know who was ordered to keep watch on them.

A man was pushed forwards by his scared fellow conscripts, and he stammered his explanation that he had kept out of sight but was sure they hadn't passed him heading south.

"And who told you they were heading south?" Renard demanded furiously in French.

The man had no answer and had to watch in abject terror as the big man made ready to throw a punch at his face.

Twenty minutes later, the boat gave up its buoyancy and with a violent hissing sound, sank to the bottom of the small dock.

Hope may have sunk, but real hope lived on, and it had headed east before turning south in an uncomfortable convoy.

THIEF IN THE NIGHT

Rich employed all of the stealth he had learned over his years spent as an elite soldier to track the twins. His ingrained skills came back naturally, the thrill of it coursing through his veins and feeling better than any drink he could have ever sipped.

He tracked them for miles in the failing light, shadowing their movements with relative ease. As the sun dipped below the horizon seven hundred miles as the crow flies away from Dan, he saw their vehicle pull off the road into a service station by the motorway.

He hid his own vehicle away from the entrance and followed on foot, moving slowly through the overgrown bushes. He moved carefully on his knees and elbows, just as he had in Afghanistan and Iraq and in the jungles of South America and in the concrete sprawl of Northern Ireland. He inched towards his target, once again the trained and proud man he knew he still was.

Inch by inch, his view expanded to encompass the large tarmac expanse of the abandoned car park until the Defender was visible, nose to nose with a big green truck. A classic British Army vehicle, one of the sights synonymous with his former life, felt homely for a second before the realisation hit him like a rubber bullet to the chest.

The twins were there, talking to a man in camouflage fatigues. He froze, watching the animated conversation as the three men gesticulated at each other. A heated discussion was obviously taking place that Rich watched in open-mouthed exasperation at what he was seeing. Lexi had been right about the twins all along: they were a plant. Double agents sent to undermine their safety and security. As it dawned on him what he was seeing, the understanding fully sunk into his alert brain.

He had to get back before them and report what he had seen. He had to have Lexi and Paul ready and armed for when they snaked back to the prison on their bellies like the serpents they truly were.

He moved back as slowly as he dared, planning to steal away in silence to his vehicle and make his egress unnoticed.

As he shuffled backwards on his belly far enough to regain his feet, a blow struck him hard across the back of the head. He went down, but not out, dropping to his knees. He lashed out viciously with his left elbow, hitting the man who had given him his best shot savagely in the groin and rendering him useless and probably sterile.

As he fought to stand up against his swimming head, blinking his eyes back into focus, another blow hit him brutally from behind, knocking him back to his knees. His retaliation was sluggish, leaving him vulnerable to a third blow.

As his face hit the ground, his hands instinctively covered his head. One, two, three barbarous kicks piled into his ribs and drove all the air from his lungs. Coughing, his hands fought to bring him back up, to fight and not go down. Lashing out with his feet, he made contact with the second attacker. A sickening crunch erupted from the knee he had struck and forced backwards against the natural movement of the joint. A scream followed the crunch, full of agony and shock. Rich fought to regain his feet and escape when a hard object hit him in the head, a rifle butt, his damaged brain later registered.

He dropped, beaten and too damaged to fight back.

"No! Get up and fight!" shouted a voice in his head. It sounded just like the evil training corporal from when he was eighteen years old and struggling to prove he was made of the stuff the Royal Marines wanted. A Royal Marine who, no matter how badly damaged, would fight all three of these bastards and kill them all.

He lashed out again, slowed by the concussion and the blood running from his lacerated scalp. Again the rifle butt smashed down on him.

He failed. Unconsciousness took him in its dark embrace.

When he came round, he was sitting up against the tall wheel of the big green truck. From his swollen lips and broken ribs, he was sure he'd received more beating after he was knocked out. *No matter*, he thought, *pain is temporary*.

Four faces looked down on him, more annoyed than angry.

"Well, this is a damned inconvenience," said the man in the crisply pressed fatigues. The insignia of an Army officer adorned his chest, and a scowl of contempt was evident on his face. "Deal with him," he said, turning his back and walking away.

The twins looked at each other, communicating without language but conveying a power struggle with their eye contact alone.

Silently, the younger of them drew his sidearm and pointed it at Rich.

Avoiding his eyes, he pulled the trigger twice and fired into his chest.

As his last bubbling, bloody breath escaped his mouth, he saw his killer turn away and holster the weapon, showing no remorse on his face.

RELAX, I'VE GOT THIS

Dan's sudden panic when he woke was only soothed when he was assured that they were safe; that the necessary precautions had been taken and the group were adequately protected.

Coffee was handed to him as he put on his kit and checked his weapons. He took the drink outside and nodded a greeting to Leah, who was lying flat on top of an abandoned vehicle to peer down the scope of the rifle towards the direction they had come from. Marie told him she had taken over from Adam just before daybreak and sent him to find somewhere to sleep.

Mitch and Neil had gone out to scout the area for anything useful.

He lit a cigarette and leaned against the side of the van under Leah's vantage point. He took a minute to tell himself it was OK, that he didn't have to do everything for everyone, and to trust in the others to make good decisions.

He had needed that six hours' sleep, desperately. Although still bone-tired, he felt better. The coffee and nicotine coursed through his body, waking him up further until he was fully alert, although more like a reanimated corpse than a rested man.

"Not to worry you or anything," came the voice from above him, "but we're being watched."

Turning and sinking to one knee, he raised the gun to scan ahead through the scope. "When will this bloody end?" he moaned to himself, having abandoned his coffee.

"Three hundred yards, left side, behind the building with the red roof," Leah calmly said to direct him to the source of her concern. That concern must have been minor, otherwise she would have been a little more vocal about the presence of another person. It was clear she had been watching them for a while.

Through his less powerful optic, he could make out the shape of a head leaning around the corner of a brick building.

"Can't see enough detail," he muttered to the girl.

The scope of the larger rifle offered far more magnification, and she filled in the information he didn't have. "Male. Young. Nervous."

"Alone?" he asked.

"Think so. What do you want to do?" she replied.

Dan thought on that. Being constantly vigilant and permanently fearful of being on unknown ground with unknown potential enemies at every turn made for a stressful existence. He wanted the chance to talk to someone local without the threat of violence or the modern-world politics of territory and possession being an obstacle.

"Where are Mitch and Neil?" he asked her.

"Gone ahead," she answered, meaning that they had gone in the opposite direction to their voyeur.

"Sod it," he said, regaining his feet and picking up his cup to drain the coffee, "cover me."

He put down the cup and gave two sharp whistles. He was rewarded seconds later by Ash bounding out to him full of expectation.

"Heel," he growled to the dog to curb his enthusiasm and began to walk slowly forwards with the carbine slung on his back so as not to look aggressive. Still, he was conscious to keep to the right side of the road and not impede Leah's line of sight should things not go well.

After a hundred yards of walking consciously as though he wasn't stalking prey, he saw the head duck out of sight. Ash saw it too and let out a low growl until Dan calmed him.

He stopped fifty paces short of the building and called out a hello.

No response. He fought to try and recall enough French to try again, but he had never mastered the language sufficiently, and tiredness didn't help his memory.

He tried again in English, this time receiving a reply.

"Wer bist du?" came a voice from behind the building.

His flash of memory at crossing over the border into Germany came back to him in a sudden rush. He was being asked who he was in a language he had a handle on.

"Wir sind aus England," he shouted back. "Wir sind freundlich!" he added to try and alleviate the obvious fear their presence had caused the man.

After a pause, the head reappeared at the corner, eliciting another growl and a change in stance from Ash. Dan quieted him again.

"Why are you here if you are from England?" came an accented question from the head.

Another revelation hit Dan then. The world over, people spoke English, which in turn made most English people fairly ignorant of other languages. Most Brits abroad relied on speaking English slowly and shouting to be understood. He knew his own grasp of German was wholly insufficient to converse with a native speaker, but thankfully this stereotypical German spoke better English than most of his group.

"Come out," Dan shouted. "We are not bad people, I swear."

Slowly, the head became a torso. The torso became a whole body and that body walked carefully towards him with his arms held high. Dan was faced with a young man, tall and thin, wearing dirty and torn clothes with a heavy bag on his back. He looked like any homeless person on any city street from before it happened, although the beard and wild hair did little to hide his youth. Dan placed him at maybe sixteen or seventeen, and was ashamed to realise that he had been sitting on the ground.

"I'm Dan," he said, "and this is Ash."

At the mention of his name and the lack of any command to attack or look threatening, Ash perked up, expecting praise and food. The way the dog switched modes made Dan think he must have a split personality. Not quite Jekyll and Hyde, but something more deliberate.

"I am Lukas," he replied, still clearly nervous.

"Nice to meet you, Lukas. Are you hungry?" he asked.

The boy's eyes lit up at the mention of food. He didn't appear to be prospering much. Dan wanted to ask him a whole raft of questions, but he knew that his "enthusiastic" manner would make that come across as an interrogation and likely scare him.

"Come on," Dan said as he turned. "Come and meet the rest of us and get something to eat."

Nervously, with a hint of resigned desperation, the boy followed him.

Leah had seen the meet-and-greet and relayed this to Marie, who was waiting for them when they arrived back at the building.

"Marie, this is Lukas," Dan said.

Almost embarrassed, Lukas's eyes flashed to hers in acknowledgement before returning to the ground. He shuffled his feet and struggled to find the words.

"It is a great pleasure to meet you," he said with a small bow of his head.

A small smile of amusement cracked Dan's face at Lukas's overly formal tone, again typical of an educated continental.

"Is breakfast ready?" Dan asked Marie as he played his part in their small pantomime.

"Almost," she replied with a smile, knowing her role in the play. "May I offer you some food?" she asked the boy, seeing his blatant hunger.

Gracefully, nervously, he accepted the kind offer with formality and was led inside.

"See," said Leah from her unnoticed perch, "you can be nice to people."

"Shut your face, you," Dan said kindly before wandering off to leave the bewildered boy to be fed and cleaned up as Leah's mocking laughter followed him.

Neil and Mitch returned thirty minutes later with the welcome news of having found a pickup truck which could take some of their equipment and offer seats to five uncomfortable passengers. The knowledge that people wouldn't have to share the windowless space with the fuel reserves was well received. Their supply situation was discussed and the decision to scout for more food and water was deemed a priority.

Perhaps, thought Dan, their recently acquired local guide could be of some assistance in that matter.

TO TRAVEL IS TO LIVE

Lukas did indeed help with local knowledge. He gave directions to shops which yielded some bottled water and more canned food. Enough to keep them going for a few more days.

The problem with that was that the space in the vehicles was even more cramped. Even more so when they agreed to add the boy to their group.

He had not fared well. He was part of his own group until a few months ago. His story was extracted carefully by Marie, and it was not a happy one. His group was small, and unlike them they had stayed in the built-up areas and scavenged far and wide. Lukas had been part of a party sent to look for more supplies when they were found by some outsiders, as he called them.

He didn't go into details, but he did say that he had hidden from the shouting and screaming, and by the time he found his way home, there was nobody left. Everyone he had lived with since it happened was either dead or taken. He had wandered ever since, for weeks or months. He couldn't be sure. It was obvious that he lacked the skills to prosper alone, but Dan doubted that many people would.

For a lack of anything better to do, he came with them. The humanitarian element overrode any sense of taking on a new mouth to feed; they simply couldn't leave the young man behind to fend for himself. He was full of formal gratitude, but painfully quiet. The women of the group fussed over him until he was cleaned up and given fresh clothes, and he joined them with a nervous smile looking like a new man.

There was little excitement over their new recruit, more a feeling of pitiful tragedy at his circumstances. How many others, Dan wondered, had similar stories? How many people could have been saved from the savagery of the new world if only his own morality were mirrored?

He pushed that thought away, scoffing at himself for believing he was a saint. There were plenty of survivors who were dead now because of his morality. Embarrassed at believing in his own flattery, he returned his thoughts to the task in hand.

The lack of preserved vehicles was a concern. By this time, everything left exposed to the elements was perished beyond their capability to repair, and they had to accept what they had.

With a subdued atmosphere, they set off towards their next objective. Paderborn. The home of the 20th Armoured Infantry Brigade, according to Mitch, with hopes of finding bigger and better vehicles and more supplies.

These hopes fought against the fear of failure inside Dan's head as he rode a sedate and alert sentry beside their overloaded convoy.

THE COUP

Lexi paced, as she did all too often recently. Only this time it was worse. She bit at her nails as her footsteps fell heavily in the small office. Paul thought she was moving fast enough for it to be classed as exercise, but he understood her stress.

He felt it too – he just didn't react like she did. He didn't have the burden of her responsibilities, for starters.

"He should be back by now," she said for the twentieth time in the last half hour. "Something's happened."

"Try and calm down," he said, instantly regretting making the fatal mistake of telling a woman under pressure to relax. The look she shot him was only fleeting, but he knew he had said the wrong thing. He fell back on logic instead. "Rich knows what he's doing. Shit, he could follow me all day and I'd never know about it," he tried.

"Exactly!" she said as she stopped pacing to point at him. "So he should be back by now. Something's happened."

Her pacing resumed.

Paul watched for another minute in silence, thinking he would have to wait out her anxiety until Rich drove back down the long drive to the house. She surprised him by snatching up the keys to the Discovery and her rifle, and she strode to the door, unable to stay still any longer.

He quickly collected his own equipment and followed her outside to hear a strange noise.

Instead of the characteristic sound of the V6 diesel sparking to life, he could hear a ticking, tortured sound. Lexi wore a frown of pure frustration from behind the wheel as she tried to start the engine again. The same strangled electrical noise sounded.

"Pop the bonnet," Paul called to her, indicating that she should pull the internal lever to allow him access to the engine bay. As he hoisted the expansive slab of metal on its hydraulic lifters, the cause of the failed start became evident.

Where the fuse box sat was a mess of wires, all torn from their allocated slots. He froze, as did Lexi when she joined him and began to ask the question she could now see the answer to.

Sabotage.

"Fuck," she said aloud, dumbstruck. She paused for a second before making straight for the front door to get another vehicle. This was her proof now; the bloody twins had sabotaged their best vehicle and now Rich was God-knows-where following them. Alone.

Her own shadow stopped her as she neared the doors. Her shadow lit from behind by vehicle lights. She turned to stare at the approaching orbs of light, hoping it was Rich returning safely.

As she stared, the realisation hit her like a punch to the chest.

Four, five sets of lights were heading straight for them.

Her mouth opened, but nothing came out. No sound, just pure abhorrent shock at what she was seeing.

Paul grabbed at her shoulder, pulling her back towards the house.

"We've got to go," he said, fear choking his words. "NOW," he shouted, dragging her away. She snapped back to reality and turned. She was vaguely aware of Paul shouting at the top of his voice to raise the house.

She didn't even try. She knew they were doomed to be overrun the second she counted the number of approaching vehicles, and she pulled on her emergency bag – her E&E kit as Dan had called it when he taught her how to use the contents. She had time to grab a few spare boxes of rifle ammunition from a shelf and throw it into the top pouch before she threw Paul's own bag at him.

"There's no time," she said, fixing him with a serious look. "We've got to go," she said hoarsely, gripping his arm.

Paul knew she was right. They could never mount a defence now, and they had maybe thirty seconds before the first vehicle pulled up on their very doorstep. He nodded, pulled on his bag and followed her to the rear doors. Lexi rounded a corner into the lounge and collided with Chris and Melissa.

"What the fuck's going on?" he asked.

"No time," she snapped at him. "Come with us now, both of you."

They both just stared at her with open mouths. Their decisions to abandon their home and their friends were taken for them as they were dragged out of the building. Only Chris resisted. He pulled his arm free of Lexi's grip and stood his ground.

"What's going on?" he snarled angrily.

"We're fucking finished, that's what's going on. In about ten seconds, someone's coming through the front door to take this place. Now fucking move," she snapped back.

Chris had no choice but to obey.

In just the clothes they wore, the four of them ran. They abandoned everyone there to the mercy of whoever was coming in superior force to take away everything they had worked to achieve. It wasn't Dan leaving that ended them; even if he and all the others were here, she doubted they could repel that many people if they were armed. The only way they had done it before was because the attack had been foiled before they could surprise them and they had a machine gun aimed at them before they knew what they were driving into.

This time, they were the ones being surprised.

This time, they would lose without a shadow of a doubt.

The four of them fled over the grass of the rear lawns and headlong into the woods. They didn't stop, not even when they heard the shouts of panic and alarm from behind them. They cut their losses, their huge and unfathomable losses, and kept running.

Roused from her sleep by the shouting, Lizzie struggled for a minute to figure out what was going on. Now that Steve was a little better, she had taken the decision to self-medicate and try to recoup some of the many hours of sleep she had lost, and the tablets made her groggy. Steve was waking up too, confused by the noise.

An armed man burst in, pointed a rifle at them and told them not to move. The instruction was easy for both of them to follow, as neither were medically able to find their feet.

She asked what was going on, only to be told to shut up. She shut up, and even shut her eyes again to return to the chemically induced sleep she was certain she was still in.

She wasn't, and slowly that realisation dawned on her.

Eyes wide in terror, she looked at Steve, trying to make eye contact and gain some form of explanation for what was happening. All around the house, shouts and screams rang out. Too terrified to move, she stayed exactly where she was and waited for her turn to endure whatever was happening to the others.

The door opened again and the twins entered. She couldn't even place their names, but she knew they looked different somehow, like they were only now seen as their true selves and had dropped whatever pretence they wore as a disguise before. Both walked tall and possessed an air of power which seemed new to her.

They were followed by a man wearing a crisp, clean uniform of camouflage material. He walked with purpose, his head held high and aloof. The man dripped with smug arrogance. He glanced at her, dismissed her immediately and walked to Steve's side.

He leaned down to stare in his eyes. Steve's pupils locked onto the man's own and widened with disbelief.

"Flight Lieutenant Bennett," he said slowly, enunciating each word carefully, "I do believe you owe me a helicopter."

With that he stood, turned on his heel and walked out.

Major Richards had promoted himself from captain after he had forcibly relocated his group. He had prospered and added numbers to his ranks with such speed that he needed a larger bureaucratic system and more junior officers to take responsibility. He had found that after amalgamating half a dozen other groups into his own. The sting of Steve's betrayal was something he refused to let go, and now he had come to swallow up the people and resources from the man who had thought to make a fool of him.

BIGGER BOY'S TOYS

Two days of careful navigation and uncomfortable travel had taken them deep into Germany. Frequent stops were needed due to their cramped conditions, and Phil's constant travel sickness had caused a medical emergency when he became so dehydrated that Kate called a stop to get potentially life-saving fluids into him by way of a drip.

As they entered the town of Paderborn, finding out the amusing news that it was twinned with Bolton in England, Dan recognised the clear evidence of an army town. Evidence to Dan, that was, having spent years in similar places. The fences were straight and neat, the roads wide and smooth. The grass was overgrown, however, and signs of disrepair were starting to creep in. Never would the British Army allow such sloppiness, he thought to himself with a wry smile.

A suitable building was found on the outskirts and a halt called for everyone to unload and relax. Dan allowed himself a brief respite as his cramped muscles burned from days spent in the saddle of an uncomfortable motorcycle. When he gauged that the others were refreshed, he took Mitch and Leah out on foot to assess their surroundings.

Moving carefully to avoid detection by the innumerable possible enemies he feared constantly, the three worked their way closer and closer to the British Forces base. Only to find it completely deserted.

Had their luck finally changed? he thought. Would they get something they needed without having to fight for it?

Like all true cynics, Dan refused to believe that such a goldmine would be totally undefended and that nobody else realised what this place held.

Ever since the end of the Second World War, the majority of the Western world's military might had been held in storage in Germany. Since before the Berlin Wall fell, throughout the height of the Cold War, the British and the Americans, mostly, had been responsible for the huge infrastructure which made it possible to roll their tanks straight into Russia at a moment's notice. Now he refused to let himself be fooled into thinking that nobody else would want what was here.

He wasn't greedy; he had no intention of taking tanks. He just wanted some well-maintained and fully fuelled trucks capable of getting them to Africa, and if he allowed himself a little artistic licence, then some new hardware wouldn't go amiss.

Forcing himself to concentrate, he ordered an observation point to be set up to watch the camp. The three of them lay still all day only a short distance apart. They saw nothing. No movement, no patrols and nothing to suggest that they couldn't walk in and take what they needed.

He made himself go slow. Watch and wait, he told himself, watch and wait.

When it neared sundown, he called the quiet withdrawal, and he and Leah returned to the others to rest and start again in the morning. Mitch, the ever-alert Mitch, offered to stay and keep watch throughout the night and promised to make radio contact at first light or in the event of a problem.

Dan knew him well enough by now to trust his instincts and have faith in his uncanny ability to go without sleep.

MILITARY DICTATORSHIP

The next three days were spent under constant guard. People were summoned, interviewed and returned to their designated holding areas until called for. Thorough searches were conducted and every item that could be used as a weapon was taken.

People were set to work loading all their carefully stockpiled supplies into a series of green Army trucks. Any questions were met with stonewalled ignorance, any dissent with instant punishment. Ewan had suffered badly, being the ill-tempered Welshman he naturally was. Lizzie had to treat him for a raft of minor injuries after he had disagreed with three of their captors, each one of them alone outweighing him and at least two heads taller.

After the second day, people started to be called by name. They were told to bring their belongings, and they were ordered into more trucks.

The farm animals were loaded into every bit of available space in their own cattle transports; those that had no space were left in situ to starve.

Richards had taken over Ops as his command post for the assimilation of the group, with his junior officers and NCOs coming in and out as tasks were issued. He was pleased with himself. He told his small army that it was their duty to take these simple people into their fold, to protect them from the harsh world and establish order.

Above all, he craved order.

"Do we have them all?" he asked a young man wearing a uniform a size too big for him.

"Sir," he stammered, "we believe that four got away, probably in the patrol vehicle we lost during the assault."

"And the two men of that patrol?" he enquired acidly.

"Don't know, sir."

Richards glared at the boy, enjoying the feeling of power as the younger man quailed under his gaze. An irritated wave of the hand dismissed the boy, prompting him to run gratefully from the room.

The victorious major leaned back in the chair, placed his feet carefully on the desk to avoid scuffing his boots that he had ordered polished to a high shine, and opened the drawer next to him. Pulling out a nearly empty bottle of single malt, he examined it with evident amusement before uncorking it and pouring the contents triumphantly into the thin carpet.

As the final stages of their hostile takeover drew to a close, he had one last event to enjoy. He rose, straightened his uniform, and strode purposefully into medical as one of the two guards posted at the door flanked him wordlessly.

"Bennett," he announced arrogantly, "don't get up." A humourless chuckle escaped his mouth as the joke he had planned came out just as he intended. He had no sense of comedic timing, due largely to the absence of any likeable traits of personality.

Steve didn't answer. As Lizzie had lost unsupervised control of their supply of medication, the pain had worsened, and a permanent prickle of sweat beaded his pale and clammy face. He lay on the bed in a constant sea of pain as Lizzie watched over him, powerless to ease his suffering.

Richards stood at the end of the bed with his hands on his hips, staring down at a broken man. "I told you that you owed me a helicopter," he said with open scorn on his face, "but I see you somewhat squandered that gift." When no answer came, he was forced to move the conversation along himself. He didn't like it when the script he had rehearsed in his head had to be altered. "I can offer you medical treatment at our new base," he said. Again, he was frustrated at receiving no answer. "But you must ask for it," he finished, leaving the humiliation heavy in the air.

Steve was in too much pain to offer any resistance. He hurt all over and felt sick with every breath. "Please," he whispered, "please."

Richards offered no answer other than to smirk again and leave the room.

ALL LIFE IS LUCK

Mitch gave a simple report as he ate the unrecognisable contents of a can of food so fast that he barely tasted it. Through his mouthfuls, he stated that there was no movement at the barracks. None. At all.

Dan thanked him, although his concentration was marred by the fact that he was unable to pull his gaze away from the slimy substance Mitch was shovelling into his mouth.

He opened his mouth to ask a sensible question about tactics when he could no longer contain himself. "What the hell are you eating?" he asked, repulsed by what he was watching.

Mitch stopped chewing, one cheek puffed out like a hamster. He looked at the can, looked back at Dan and offered a shrug.

Shaking his head to clear the image from his brain, Dan returned to the task. "Get your head down for a few hours," he said, looking away to hide his disgust.

He moved around the others, "doing the rounds," as he called it. Taking a lap around the group, exchanging pleasantries and cracking bad dad jokes reminded him why they were all going through this hardship: they were a family. A large, highly dysfunctional one with a family pet who would most certainly raise complaints from the neighbours, but they were still a family.

That afternoon, they carefully approached the front gates of the base and opened them unopposed. Moving his small team of makeshift soldiers, drivers and engineers into the series of large buildings, he marvelled at the sheer size of the place. Row upon row of challenger tanks waited inside a unit the size of an aircraft hangar. Another held a swathe of armoured vehicles with their wire blast netting protruding awkwardly. It was difficult for most of them to stay focused; they were unchaperoned children in a sweet shop. It was like a backstage pass.

The rest of the day was spent picking their new fleet. A huge supply truck with a large cab and rows of seats in the back became Jack's new prized possession. An off-road truck, the likes of which Dan had never seen, was claimed by Neil, a double cab with a fuel tank dominating the rear of the chassis.

A whistle from Mitch towards the rear of the building made Dan jog up to where he and Leah were standing, both of them grinning like children. He could excuse that from Leah, obviously.

Dan's own face cracked into a smile, instantaneously transforming the scowling look he bore because of the scar into one of pure childlike joy.

"It's called a Foxhound," Mitch said proudly.

Dan walked a slow circle around the resting beast. It was like his old Discovery on steroids. A v-shaped hull gave it an aggressive stance. He opened the rear doors – the only way inside the protective cocoon – and saw four seats in the back as well as two up front.

"We were suffering badly from roadside bombs in Iraq and Afghanistan," explained Mitch, "so this was developed to replace the Land Rovers we were using. Four-wheel steering too."

Dan had heard enough. It was his; it had to be. Bulletproof and blastproof, all feelings of loss for the comfortable 4x4 he had left behind evaporated.

Leah smiled at him.

"Shotgun," she called out with a smirk.

Sending Jack, Adam, and Neil back with the big supply truck to fetch the rest of the group, they set about deciding what else to take and where to search for more supplies.

The camp was huge. They avoided the barrack blocks for no other reason than they didn't want to find the skeletons of so many men and women, but stores were found and stockpiles of uniform raided.

Over the next two days, they stripped down everything they carried, replaced their own equipment with better items and gathered their strength. Try as they might, nothing they had with them could bypass the physical security to access the weapons lockers.

In terms of firepower, they had to make do with what they had. Luckily, that was still quite a lot. Dan marvelled that they had travelled all this distance and the only shots fired were for hunting, but that was a matter of luck too, he guessed.

Refreshed, replenished, and in far more safety and comfort than before, they prepared to resume their journey south.

Leading the way in his Foxhound with Leah beside him, he glanced over his shoulder at Lukas and Marie as Ash nosed his way in between the two front seats to get a good view of the road ahead. They were followed by the large transport truck bearing the majority of the group as well as box upon box of ration packs; the store of MREs caused great delight, as most of them had never eaten out of a self-heating tinfoil bag before.

Behind them came Neil's tanker, fully stocked with diesel full of additives to prolong the life of the fuel. That was another thing Dan hadn't realised; he never thought to question the sell-by date on fuel, but Mitch assured him that the stocks on the bases were full of chemicals to keep them viable, as they were a stockpile and not an everyday use.

At the tail came Mitch with Adam beside him, a tried and tested military Snatch Land Rover similar to their old Defenders bringing up the rear.

Armed, armoured, and well equipped, they rolled south towards Munich.

Only to find the road barred not three miles away.

EPILOGUE

"If we stay here, then they'll find us," Lexi hissed at the other three from the deep cover of the woodland they hid in.

Nobody could counter that with any feasible logic.

"We've got to get away from here," she finished, taking control for the first time since Dan had left.

Moving as carefully as they could still made every footfall sound like a firework display as the dried and broken branches snapped under their boots. Melissa cried quietly while Chris remained silent.

It took them an hour to move through the darkness around the lake to find the blocked access road leading back to the tarmac. The rusting hulks of the vehicles dumped there by Ewan after the last attack on their home loomed ahead.

Crouching by the side of a wreck, Lexi listened intently. Leaning back to Paul, she told him what she knew. "Voices. At least two men," she said.

Paul nodded and switched places with her. He watched through the darkness, seeing the flash of a lighter as one of them lit a cigarette. He listened for a few minutes before turning back. "Two of them, and they have a vehicle," he said.

Lexi thought for a minute. "No guns," she said, unslinging her rifle and handing it to Chris as she whispered for them to stay put.

Lexi had never followed suit and equipped herself with a suppressed weapon, suddenly regretting that decision. A gunshot would bring their attackers down on them, something that none of them wanted. Paul did the same, handing his own rifle to Melissa, who held it as though it would explode at any moment.

As slowly as they could, Lexi and Paul crept out of their hiding place and inched towards the two bored sentries. Being given the perimeter cordon was a job for the lame and the lazy, it seemed, as the two did nothing but complain about their allocated task.

One was sitting in the passenger side of a car, carelessly bathing himself in the soft yellow light. He would be completely blind to anything over two paces away, whereas their own night vision was well attuned by now. The other played it perfectly for them.

"I need a piss," he announced to his dull-witted partner as he wandered away into the undergrowth.

He passed only a few feet away from Paul, who struck like a snake. Rising from his crouch, he wrapped his left arm tightly around the man's neck and pulled him tight to his body. With his right hand, he pulled the opposite side of his head painfully down.

No sound could escape his mouth, and Paul dropped his body weight into the back of his knees to take him down. Leaning back, he exerted every ounce of pressure he could muster, the long hours of his life spent lifting weights suddenly meaning the difference between life and death. The combination of the force on his head pressing the bony part of his left wrist into the side of the man's neck made his struggles short-lived.

With a massive effort that betrayed Paul's sheer strength, he violently twisted the man's head towards him. The sickening sound of a

216

single, sinuous crunch died away in the following silence. Breathing heavily, Paul gently laid the dead man down.

The lazy one in the car was still complaining. When he didn't receive any verbal ratification for his complaints, he called out to his partner.

Receiving only silence in return, he climbed out of the lit interior of the car and tried to blink away his immediate blindness.

Movement flashed in front of him, and still he failed to react. A blonde woman appeared from the dark and hit him hard in the chest with a knee. He slammed back into the car and drew breath to shout an alarm when he was struck hard in the throat and a red-hot burning sensation exploded in his groin.

Lexi drove her knife hilt first into his windpipe, then reversed it and plunged the blade into the inside of his hip joint where it met the top of his fleshy thigh. Struggling to hold her hand over his mouth, she sawed the knife backwards and forwards until rewarded by a pressurised spurt of hot blood. Holding him there, she watched the life drain almost instantly from his eyes as she let go to watch him slump to the floor.

Paul joined her, saw what she had done and placed a hand on her shoulder.

"We need to go," he whispered again, running back to fetch the others.

Lexi nodded to him, even though he had already gone. Wiping her hand and her knife on her victim, she began removing his weapons before dragging his body away to the bushes to hide it with the other.

Paul had retrieved similar weapons from the man he had killed and all four piled into the car. Setting off slowly, he drove for over an hour in near darkness before he stopped.

He killed the engine to save fuel as silence hung heavy in the car.

"So, what do we do now?" asked Melissa from the back in a small voice.

"We go south," replied Paul. "We go south, we cross the Channel, and we find the others.

The story continues in AFTER IT HAPPENED BOOK 5: SANCTUARY

A message from the author

Thanks for reading. Please leave a review on Amazon if you enjoyed it!

You can find me on:

    Twitter: @DevonFordAuthor

    Facebook: Devon C Ford Author

Subscribe to my email list and read my blog:

    www.devonfordauthor.uk